D0498170

STRIKER

DAVID SKUY

JAMES LORIMER & COMPANY LTD., PUBLISHERS
TORONTO

Copyright © 2013 by David Skuy
First published in the United States in 2014.

All rights reserved. No part of this book may be reproduced or transmitted in any form or by any means, electronic or mechanical, including photocopying, or by any information storage or retrieval system, without permission in writing from the publisher.

James Lorimer & Company Ltd., Publishers acknowledges the support of the Ontario Arts Council. We acknowledge the financial support of the Government of Canada through the Canada BookFund for our publishing activities. We acknowledge the support of the Canada Council for the Arts which last year invested $24.3 million in writing and publishing throughout Canada. We acknowledge the Government of Ontario through the Ontario Media Development Corporation's Ontario Book Initiative.

Cover design: Meredith Bangay
Cover image: iStock

Library and Archives Canada Cataloguing in Publication

Skuy, David, 1963-, author
　　Striker / David Skuy.

Issued in print and electronic formats.
ISBN 978-1-4594-0512-7 (bound).--ISBN 978-1-4594-0513-4 (pbk.).--
ISBN 978-1-4594-0514-1 (epub)

　　I. Title.

PS8637.K72S87 2013　　jC813'.6　　C2013-904181-8
C2013-904182-6

James Lorimer & Company Ltd.,
Publishers
317 Adelaide Street West, Suite 1002
Toronto, ON, Canada
M5V 1P9
www.lorimer.ca

Distributed in the United States by:
Orca Book Publishers
P.O. Box 468
Custer, WA, USA
98240-0468

Printed and bound in Canada.
Manufactured by Friesens Corporation in Altona, Manitoba, Canada
in August 2013.
Job #87634

A sincere thanks to all the kids who have continued to read (and correct) my work over the years — hopefully we can keep going!

Cody fought the urge to rub the back of his right leg. His mom got crazy worried if he so much as scratched — only, it was really tight and it hurt. The doctor said it would feel better in time, the one thing he didn't have. He'd already missed one season because of the tumour. He couldn't miss another.

He folded his arms across his chest and rolled the soccer ball back and forth with his foot. The tryout was in two days. He had to ask his mom to let him play — it was now or never.

"Have you thought about soccer much lately?" he said, as if he was asking about the weather.

"I haven't had time to think about anything," his mom said. She rifled through a pile of papers on her desk, and then scrolled down the computer screen. "Where is that ridiculous file?"

Cody rolled the ball a little faster. "I mean, have you thought about me . . . and soccer. 'Cause the season is starting, and . . ."

"I can't believe this. It disappeared. Twenty minutes wasted." She ran a hand through her hair.

His mom was obviously stressed about work. Definitely not prime time to ask if she would let him try out for a rep team. "I think I might go play a bit . . . outside . . . maybe at the park. You know the one, not far . . . just down the street."

She took her glasses off. "I know where the park is. But do you have to go now? I'm right in the middle of something. Give me half an hour, and I'll drive you."

"I don't need a drive to the park."

"It's fine. Give me a few minutes, and I'll take you."

"I can go myself."

"Don't be silly. It's a far walk."

"It's five minutes."

"Cody. The doctor said you need to take it easy. Your last treatment was less than a month ago. You'll tire out . . . and what if you fell and got hurt and I wasn't there . . . or . . . It's thirty minutes. Please wait. I just need to find this file." Her phone rang. "Yes, Suzanna. I can't find it. It's maddening . . ."

Cody dribbled the ball out of the room. Typical! This treating him like a little kid. Thirteen years old and he couldn't even go to the park without his mommy. "Even you want to go, don't ya, Mr. Ball?" he said. He gave the ball a soft kick and it rolled the length of the hall to the front door. Then he rubbed the back of his right thigh.

Hard to believe what happened because he'd felt a lump eight months ago.

Cody went over and picked the ball up, spinning it in his hands. It was a bad idea; he knew it. But it wouldn't go away. The more he heard his mom talking on the phone to her boss, the more he felt the urge to give in, as if some powerful wizard had cast a spell over him. He took his skullcap from the hook and quietly opened the front door.

The air was cool, even for a late spring day. Sweatshirt weather, for sure, but going back was way too risky. His mom would hear him. She'd said she needed thirty minutes, and he'd be back before then. He could tell she didn't really feel like going, anyway; and this wasn't technically lying. She hadn't said he couldn't go by himself. He began to jog slowly, controlling the ball with his insteps.

The park was a bit further than five minutes away. He promised himself that he'd stay for only ten minutes, and then hightail it back. It was deserted, anyway, other than a couple of older kids playing basketball — not exactly a ton of fun.

Cody dropped the ball to the grass and began to bounce it up in the air. He got to seven touches before it fell.

"That was pathetic, Cody," he told himself. He was so out of practice.

The next time he got to ten, and then twelve. On the fourth try the ball nicked his toe and bounded toward the court. Cody adjusted his skullcap and shuffled over. His head was sweaty but he wasn't about to freak everyone out at the park with his bald head. Dr. Charya said that would take time too — like everything else!

The *thud – thud – thud* of the bouncing basketball interrupted his thoughts.

"Yo. Deaf one. Wake up. Toss me the ball."

A tough-looking kid, his jet-black hair swooped to the
side and cut close to his head, pointed at a large evergreen
tree. The basketball was under a branch. Cody felt himself flush. He always got scared around big kids, and this
guy didn't seem too friendly. Cody threw it over. The kid
caught it and without a word of thanks began dribbling.

"Can't stop me, Stick," he jeered. "You ain't got the
game."

Stick was a good nickname, Cody thought. The friend
was tall and skinny.

"Big talk, Trane. You ain't hit nothin' all day."

Trane cross-dribbled to his left and drove hard to the
basket, banging his shoulder into Stick's chest. Trane was
bigger, and Stick bounced back a few steps. Trane laid the
ball up for an easy hoop.

"Total foul," Stick protested.

Trane passed him the ball. "That's called a power move,
loser. Get used to it. Or do you need a diaper change?"

Stick whipped the ball back and Trane caught it smoothly and laid it up again.

"Count another two," he said.

Cody drifted away, tapping his ball off the outsides of
his feet. He soon heard a sound far more to his liking. A
kid on the other side of the basketball court, much smaller
than Trane or Stick, was playing soccer by himself. He was
good, too. He bounced the ball off one foot so many times
Cody lost count. Then he began alternating feet, and the

ball stayed up even when he walked forward. Cody had never seen a little kid with such skills. Finally, the kid tried kicking it high and doing a spin; he almost pulled it off, only the ball skidded off the side of his foot and bounced across the court.

The kid ran to get it. As he grabbed his ball, Trane backed into him.

"Watch what you're doing, doofus? Get off my court," Trane said. He ripped the soccer ball out of the kid's hands.

"Thanks for the ball, loser," he laughed, tossing it to Stick.

"Give it back," the kid yelled. He had an accent.

"What jungle are you from?" Trane taunted.

The kid balled his fists. "I ain't from no jungle, idiot. Give me my ball."

"Or what?"

The kid lunged for the ball. Stick threw it to Trane. The kid charged for it again. Trane tucked the ball under his arm, caught the kid by the back of his shirt and in one motion spun him around and tossed him to the ground. The kid jumped right back. Trane threw the ball to Stick, and then, holding him by the arm, dragged the kid off the court and threw him toward a garbage can.

"Next time I'll put you in it," Trane growled, "so get lost." He turned as if to go back to the court but then whirled around and added, "And why don't you go back where you came from?" He called out to Stick, "Let's see my new ball." Stick bounce passed it. Trane whistled in admiration. "Nice ball — looks expensive." He pointed to the kid. "Now beat it or I'm gonna rearrange your face for real."

11

Trane and Stick began kicking the ball to each other. Cody slowly backed away, keeping an eye on the kid as he disappeared behind some trees that bordered the tennis courts. Cody wanted to help. But what could he do?

After a minute or so, Trane called out, "This is bogus. Let's get back to some B-ball." He rolled the soccer ball to the side and he and Stick began to play one-on-one again.

Cody sat on his ball. He could imagine how bad the kid felt. Then, just like when he'd been talking to his mom, another crazy idea popped into his head. Trying to look bored, his heart pounding harder and harder with each step, he ambled over to the side of the court.

He desperately hoped he looked natural and that Trane and Stick would ignore him, but he found it harder and harder to breathe and sweat was dripping from under his skullcap. He glanced as nonchalantly as he could to his left. Trane was dribbling to the basket, Stick pushing and shoving to keep him outside of the key. In one motion, Cody scooped up the boy's soccer ball.

Now his heart was pounding so hard he was sure Trane and Stick would hear it!

"Two points for the king," Trane exclaimed.

"Two lucky points for the Turd King," Stick answered.

Cody wasted no time retrieving his own ball — it was an old one, anyway. As fast as he could without looking too obvious he headed for the tennis courts. The kid was nowhere to be seen, though. Cody walked around to the back where a thicket of trees and bushes obscured the view down to a ravine.

A hand grabbed his shoulder. "Do you have it?"

Cody jumped back. The kid had followed him.

He was greeted by a wide smile and gleaming white teeth. "Sorry about that. I guess I kinda scared you. But I saw you get my ball." The kid's eyes flashed eagerly.

He was smaller than Cody but he looked about the same age. Cody took a deep breath. His shoulders relaxed, and he dropped the ball to the ground. The kid drew it back with his foot, and then flicked it up into his hands.

"Thanks. Those guys are total jerks. This is my dad's ball and he would've been mad if I'd come home without it."

"It's a sweet ball, for sure," Cody said.

"It's from Brazil," he said proudly.

Cody didn't know what to say next — probably just goodbye. He wasn't going back to the park, not with Trane and Stick there; and he was nervous about how long he'd stayed already. "Yeah . . . Well . . . Glad to help. Take it easy — and I'd stay away from those guys. They're pretty big."

He shrugged. "I'm not afraid of them. I play where I want."

Cody had to laugh — he believed him. The kid didn't seem scared one bit.

"What's your name?"

The sudden question startled Cody. "Um . . . It's Cody." He paused. "What's yours?"

"Paulo."

"Cool. So . . . See ya . . . Paulo."

"See ya, Cody." He paused. "How old are you?"

"Thirteen."

"Me, too." Paulo flashed his wide toothy grin. "I play

soccer a lot. I live down on the other side of the ravine. We should kick the ball around some time. I was watching you. You're a good player."

Cody blushed. He was nothing compared to Paulo. "Sure — sounds good. I'll see y'around. Bye."

Cody cut across the field, careful to stay as far from the basketball court as he could. On a whim, he turned to wave, but Paulo had already headed down the hill and was out of sight. He felt good about what he'd done. Soccer players had to stick together!

He wondered if he'd see Paulo again.

His mom's cheeks were streaked with tears. His dad stood
behind her with his hand on her shoulder. Cody wished
he'd stayed at the park.

"I was so worried I almost called the police," his mom
said. "You're so selfish, Cody. Think of how I felt. Is it too
much to ask for you to wait twenty minutes?"

"I think you said something like thirty," Cody said.

"Do not joke about this, mister," she snapped.

"I wasn't," he said quickly. "I just meant I didn't want
to bother you . . . and it was going to take a long time and
. . . I'm really sorry, Mom. I just went down the street to
the corner and back, just to stretch the leg. Felt awesome,
too. Really awesome. Totally awesome . . . Anyway, it was
fine, and I came right back."

"Do you understand the issue, Cody?" his dad said. He

seemed more tired than angry. His mom had called him on his cell when she discovered Cody wasn't in the house and he'd raced home.

"I do understand, and I'm really, really, sorry. It was a dumb thing to do. I got so stoked about getting out and playing . . ."

His dad nodded. "I can accept that. As long as you realize how upset you made your mother."

She wiped her eyes with a tissue. "At least tell me where you're going," she said, sighing deeply. "You know the rules."

"Sorry, Mom. I will."

She held her arms wide, and he leaned his head on her shoulder as she pulled him in for a hug. It was a long time before she let him go.

He'd chickened out of asking her so many times he couldn't believe how the words tumbled out all of a sudden. "I found out about a soccer team, Mom. They practise really close . . . like, ten minutes away by car at the most. I asked dad about it and he said it would be okay and that . . . and . . . it's a new team, I think, their first year in the Major division, which is what I played last year . . . or the season before . . . before I got the cancer."

"We don't use that word," his mom said sharply.

"Right. Sorry. Anyway. The tryouts start this weekend, on Saturday, and I was thinking I should try out and maybe make it, and then I could play . . . soccer, I mean."

He stopped suddenly, not sure if he had made much sense.

His mom's eyebrows were raised — a very bad sign.

16

"You spoke to your father about this before me?"

Not the question he'd expected. "I did a little, about the driving and stuff."

"Sean. Were you going to involve me in this decision?"

"Of course, Cheryl. I was . . . I've been working late this week, and it slipped my mind . . ."

"Slipped your mind," she exploded. "Your son wants to risk his health and do something as crazy as play competitive soccer again so soon after . . ." Her fists were balled tightly and she punched the air as she spoke. "You remember we have a son who needs to be very careful; he's the priority, not work."

Cody felt his stomach tighten. His mom was always yelling at his dad about working too much, and maybe he did. He spent a ton of time at the office or doing paperwork at home.

"I think I remember we have a son," his dad said calmly. "In fact, I left a meeting to come here when you called."

That tone of voice meant he was angry. He seemed to be angry about something or other a lot of the time.

"Then prove it," she snapped. "And as for you," she added, turning back to Cody, "there will be no soccer this summer. Don't be ridiculous. I mean, really. What were you two thinking?"

"Not sure if one tryout will be so bad," his dad said.

"Not too bad! Not too bad! You know what the doctor said."

"I believe she said Cody should try to get back to normal."

"Playing sports is not normal. He's not ready."

They were talking as if he weren't even in the room. He couldn't hold it in. "I'm not allowed to do anything, then. I just have to spend the rest of my life watching everyone else have fun. Thanks, Mom. Why don't you lock me in my bedroom and feed me with a baby spoon."

"That's obviously not what we want," his dad said.

"Then why can't I play soccer? I did before I got . . ."

"I do not want to hear that word," his mom said. "That's over and in the past."

"It's not over," Cody fumed. "You're not cured for five years, and the cancer can come back. We all know that."

"Cody!" his dad said.

"No, it won't," his mom cried. "How can you say that? I won't listen to that."

"I don't get the big deal. I had cancer. I had an operation to remove a tumour from my leg. Cancer is just a word — like pizza."

"Not exactly the same thing, Cody," his dad said.

His mom closed her eyes and breathed in deeply. "Cody, you know how much we love you. My goodness, this has been so hard on all three of us. We had to sell the house and move to be close to the hospital, and you missed the last six months of school, not to mention Daddy has a longer drive to work . . ."

"I didn't mind that," his dad said.

She waved him off. "The point is we're all in this together. It's not about me; it's about what's best for your health. Next year I'd love for you to play. You know how much I enjoy watching you. How many practices and games have I sat through?"

Cody put his hand to his forehead. "I'm fine now, Mom. I was just at the park and walked around no problem."

"You went to the park?" she said. "I thought you only went to the corner."

"I meant the corner."

"Cody?"

Soccer was over. He knew it. May as well come clean. "I went to the park to kick the ball around and test my leg. I knew you wouldn't let me if I asked. Sorry. But I had to. And I was fine, by the way."

"I would have taken you," his mom said.

"And you would've had a heart attack if I'd ran faster than a turtle, and you know it."

"Cody, you may be upset, but let's not be rude," his dad said.

"Mom's being crazy overprotective. Soccer isn't going to make the cancer come back."

"Don't say that word!" she said.

"Then don't say I can't play soccer until next summer. It's not so easy to make a rep team, and if I miss this season I won't have the skills. It's been forever since I played, and this is the only team at the Major level that practises near us. The other teams are too far away."

His dad put up his hand "Hold on, you two. I have an idea." He looked at Cody. "When is the tryout, again?"

"Saturday afternoon — three o'clock."

"And how long is it?"

"Two hours, I guess."

"So that gives us two days to see how your leg feels after your run in the park. We can all go tomorrow and test it out again, too." He turned to his mom. "Cheryl, one tryout won't be a problem. If his leg hurts, either after a run in the park or at any time during the tryout, then absolutely I say that's the end. But . . . what's the harm in giving it a shot?"

Cody pleaded with his eyes. Would she let him — this one time?

"I worry too much. I know that," she said softly. Cody allowed himself to hope. "I also know you love to play soccer and you're good at it." The briefest of smiles appeared. "You forget sometimes that I'm also a soccer player."

That was true. She'd been good enough to play at university on a scholarship.

His mom crossed her arms and she sat up straight. "If anything happened to you I'd never forgive myself. I just think it's too soon."

Cody felt a tear fall down his cheek.

His dad leaned forward. Here comes the "Don't worry about it" speech, Cody thought. Dad always gave in to her.

But he surprised Cody this time.

"It's only one tryout, Cheryl. We'll both go, and if you see any problem . . ."

Her shoulders sagged. "You two are relentless." A few seconds passed. "Fine. Go. But I'm not watching," his mom said. "I can't. You have to take him, Sean. And if anything happens, I swear, I'll never . . ."

"Nothing will happen," Cody practically shouted. He couldn't control the huge smile that burst out across his face. "Thanks, Mom. I feel great — never better. You should've seen me running around the park like a maniac."

"Now you were running around?"

"I didn't really; it's just a . . . I didn't mean that . . . I ran to the tennis courts and back."

She held out her arms, and he dutifully laid his head on her shoulder.

"We'll get through this together. Don't worry. Things will all be better soon," she said, rocking him side to side.

He tried to pull away but she wouldn't let go. Cody began to feel silly, all bent over; he also had a feeling that his mom was crying. He waited a bit longer, and then began to wiggle out of her arms.

She let go and wiped away her tears. "I'm sorry I love you so much. I can't help it."

"I know, Mom. It's just . . ." He wanted to tell her to let him be a kid again, even though he'd had cancer, that he'd never feel healthy until he could play soccer again, and that the doctor had told him not to let the cancer control him. But looking at the expression on his mom's face, he figured that could wait for another day.

"Can I go soak my leg in the bath? I'm supposed to do it once a day . . ."

"Of course, honey. Do you want me to run the water for you?" She got up.

"No, that's okay. I'll do it." His mom would probably stay in the bathroom and talk to him. "I feel like reading . . . by myself."

"Excellent idea," his dad said.

"Okay. If you need anything, just holler," his mom said.

"Will do," Cody said. He stepped toward the hallway—and felt a sharp pain sweep up his right leg. A groan escaped his lips.

"Cody?"

"My leg just fell asleep when I was sitting. I'm good. No problem. Look." He jumped up and down a few times, ignoring the tightness that ran up his leg each time he landed.

"Go soak, Mr. Jumping Jack," his mom said.

He managed not to limp until he got out of the kitchen and turned the corner. Then he hopped on his left foot to the stairs and, using the handrail for balance, hauled himself up. The doctor had said his leg would be very stiff and feel weak when he started to move around on it. That was probably it, just a little stiff. A hot bath, and he'd be fine.

Cody turned on the water, and then ran his finger slowly along the scar where they'd taken out the tumour. His right leg was really skinny compared to his left. He had to get to the park tomorrow and stretch and run around a bit more. He'd never make the team with his leg like this.

And he had to make that team.

On the sidelines, clipboard in hand, a tall, sturdy-looking man was calling out names and pointing to different parts of the pitch. His dad was still parking, and for a moment Cody wanted to run back to him. What would the other kids say when he took his skullcap off, or they saw his scar or his skinny leg? Then the man spotted Cody and waved at him.

He was dressed in black track pants and a yellow T-shirt with *Lions* written across the chest. The man took off his hat to reveal a few strands of blackish-grey hair and wiped his forehead with a towel. The hat was black also, with a dragon emblem stitched in yellow on one side and a picture of a lion with the words *Lions FC* written below on the other.

In a booming voice the man asked, "Now, who do we have here, young man?"

"I'm Cody Dorsett, sir."

"And I'm Ian Henning, manager of the Lions Football Club and the team sponsor. Good to meet you, Cody. Please feel free to call me Ian." He looked at his clipboard and checked something on the page. "I'll put you on Team Four with Timothy. If you get in trouble with the ball, give it to him. Cool?"

Cody figured Timothy was the team star. He nodded.

"Now, what position do you play?

"I'm a striker."

Ian's eye's got big. "We already have our strikers, so . . . Anyway, take off your sweats and that . . ." he paused, "that hat . . . and warm up. Coach Henry will talk to everyone in a few minutes."

"Okay. Thanks."

He walked toward the pitch.

"Excuse me," Ian said. "There's a twenty-five-dollar fee for the tryout. I pay for a lot of stuff but this pitch still costs something to rent." He laughed.

Cody had no idea why that was funny. "My dad is parking. He'll pay you."

Ian wrapped his towel around his neck. "Awesome. Have a good practice . . ." He looked at his clipboard, ". . . Cody."

Four men dressed in the same track pants, T-shirt, and hat came over. One of them also had a clipboard. "I've got thirty-eight kids trying out, with four goalies," the man with the clipboard said to Ian.

Cody drifted away. That was a lot of kids, and Ian had said the strikers were already chosen. What was he going to do? He'd always been a striker, never played another position except when he was a little kid in house league. But he'd have to do something or else he wouldn't have a chance to make the team. He noticed a ball bounding toward him and he skipped over a few steps to trap it before it rolled off the pitch.

"Nice stop," a kid yelled. He came over. "You're trying out, right?"

Cody nodded.

"Come on, then. Let's warm up."

Cody flicked the ball back. The kid showed some skills by stopping it easily with his left foot.

"You gonna take off all your stuff? You'll melt under all that gear."

Cody pulled his sweats off. He closed his eyes for a moment to prepare himself, and then took off his skullcap. He could tell the kid noticed though he didn't say anything. He just hoofed the ball to another player and waited for Cody, and together they jogged onto the pitch.

"So where'd you play last year?"

This kid sure was friendly. "I hurt my leg and had to sit out, so I didn't really play much."

"That's a pain. Can't imagine missing an entire season. You must be totally stoked to start up again. How's the leg?"

"It's okay, I guess — a bit stiff. I haven't tested it out much."

The kid waved his hand over his head. "Luca, send one over."

Luca was a powerful-looking kid, a little short but with big shoulders. He passed his ball.

"There you go. Test away," he said.

A wave of anxiety swept over Cody. All he'd done in the park with his parents yesterday was run around and pass the ball back and forth with his mom. He hadn't kicked a ball hard in ages and he certainly wasn't going to risk kicking with his right leg now. He collected himself with a deep breath, took two steps, and with his left foot blasted the ball back to Luca. It flew way over his head.

The kid laughed. "The leg seems good to me — maybe too good."

"That's not the one I hurt," Cody said.

The kid laughed again. "I'm Kenneth. We may as well introduce ourselves if we're gonna be teammates."

"I haven't made the team yet."

He slapped Cody's back, laughing all the while. "I got confidence in you; it's me I'm worried about." He waited a moment. "So . . . what's your name?"

"I'm Cody," he said. "Did you play on the Lions last year?"

"Nah. I'm making the big jump to Major, along with my bud Luca."

A piercing whistle interrupted them. Most of the guys headed to midfield, where a grey-haired man wearing a snug, white soccer jersey was waving to them.

"I think the fun's about to start," Kenneth said. He cupped his hands around his mouth and yelled, "Hey, Luca, come here." Then to Cody he said, "So what position do you play, anyway?"

"I'm a striker . . . At least, that's what I usually play."

Kenneth's smile, which never left his face, got even bigger.

"Perfect," he said. "I'm a midfielder, and Luca is a

defender. Together we got the whole pitch covered." Kenneth pointed at Cody. "This here is the most dangerous striker in the league. I believe he calls himself Cody."

"Then that's what I'll call him," Luca said. "You ready to go hard? This is going to be a tough tryout, for sure."

"I guess I'd better if I want to make it."

"You need to focus on those two over there," Luca said, pointing at two players standing next to Ian and a couple of the men wearing the dragon hats. "The big guy with the red hair is Timothy, leading scorer last year." He held a hand to the side of his mouth and lowered his voice. "I might score a lot, too, if I shot every time I touched the ball."

Kenneth snorted. "You ain't never scored a goal in your life."

Luca gave him a good-natured shove. "The other kid is John. Their dads are the team managers. They're both strikers, but that should leave at least one spot for you."

So there was a chance, after all. He might not start, but all he really cared about was making the team and getting back into soccer. Timothy and John couldn't play every minute of every game.

The three boys walked to centre and knelt. The grey-haired man folded his arms, pressing a small whiteboard to his chest. "Boys, my name is Henry Bowman. Welcome. I know tryouts are hard on everyone. I hate them, and I really hate making cuts. But we can only carry eighteen players according to league rules, so . . . that's life."

He spoke softly, and the dark circles under his eyes made him look tired and even a little sad.

"As you must know, this team is moving up a division

27

to Major, which means we're going to have to adjust our style. In Major the ball moves faster and it's more of a team game. We need to work on ball control and quick passes. It'll be a lot of work, but it'll be fun, too. I can promise you that. To warm up, let's divide into our four teams and do some stretching . . ."

Ian stepped forward. "You've all met me, I think," he said loudly. "I'm Ian Henning, team manager and the main sponsor." He elbowed John's dad. "This here is Mitch. He's the assistant manager. Those three cats over there are the other sponsors, and they help organize things, too."

The three men waved to the boys. Two of them punched fists. Cody heard a man say, "The Dragons are in the house!"

Ian grinned. "You'll be hearing a lot of that this season. We five call ourselves the Dragons and we make sure things run smoothly — that you have the practice time and game preparation you need to win. And, believe me, our goal is to win every game, every tournament, and the league championship. Nothing's going to stop us. Last year we made it to the finals — and lost 'cause of some unbelievably stupid calls by the ref."

"Refs are usually dumb. This one was blind, too," Timothy said.

John and a few others around him laughed loudly, as did the Dragons.

"Ancient history," Ian continued, "even though we were totally robbed in that game, in my humble opinion. I'm glad to see most of the same guys from last year are out. That leaves a few positions open to newcomers, so give it your best. We'll be watching every move; don't let up. We play a relentless, aggressive style of soccer." A smile played across his face. "I hope you new kids are in shape, because you don't stop running on this team." He flashed a thumbs-up. "We only have the field for ninety minutes, Henry, so I want to get the boys scrimmaging as much as possible to evaluate the new talent. I think they're warmed up, so let's get right to it."

Henry gripped his whiteboard with both hands. "We really should have them warm up as a group."

"It'll be fine," Ian said. "We need to start scrimmaging."

"Five or ten minutes won't hurt," Henry said.

"Time is money," Mitch said.

"Let's see what these boys can do," another Dragon added.

"Boys, I need Teams One and Two at the far end of the pitch," Ian said. "Mitch will ref your game. Teams Three and Four go to the other end. I'll ref that one. Okay? Let's move it." He looked to Henry. "Give me a whistle to signal the start of practice," he said.

Henry walked away.

Ian watched him for a few paces, and then pointed to Mitch. "Can you do the honours?"

Mitch lifted the whistle hanging around his neck to his lips and gave it a blow. It barely made a sound.

"Nice whistle," a Dragon said.

"Now give it a big-boy try," Ian said.

Mitch had turned a deep red. He blew and blew, and finally the whistle came to life.

"Awesome work," Ian said laughing.

The players began to head to their respective ends. "What team are you on?" Kenneth asked him.

"Team Four," Cody said.

"Too bad," Kenneth said, making a sour face. "Me and Luca are on Team Two. See you after the scrimmage." They headed to their end.

Cody was disappointed. He'd only just met those guys, but it would've been nice to be on their team. Less intimidating. He scanned the sidelines for his dad quickly, and then gave up. He was probably still in the car, doing work. He headed to the far end.

"Hurry up," Ian yelled. "We don't have all day. Team Three to my left — and you can figure out where Team Four goes." He laughed loudly.

"Listen up, girls," a kid said in a mean voice. Timothy was counting the players on Team Four. John stood next to him.

Cody's heart sank. He was playing with the two best strikers.

"We got eight players and a goalie," Timothy continued. "Me and J-Man will be up front. Who wants midfield?" Midfield was the obvious choice after striker, Cody figured; he could join the attack. He put up his hand. Timothy didn't seem to notice him and picked three other players.

"Awesome," Timothy said. "That leaves three defenders." He nodded at Cody. "Where do you play?"

Cody flushed. "I'm actually a striker, so . . ."

Timothy rolled his eyes. "Egg-Head has trouble hearing," he said.

The whistle blew.

"That's enough time," Ian called out. "Line up, already."

"You guys work out the back line," Timothy said, and he and John ran to centre.

Most of the guys stared at him as they spread out across the pitch. He had to force himself to stay; if he'd seen his dad he might have left right then and there. *Egg-Head* — was that how it was gonna be? A tap on his shoulder startled him.

"I'll play middle. Do you wanna take right back?" a boy asked him.

Cody nodded gratefully and took his spot. Dumb of him to tell Timothy that he was a striker; of course there'd be a comment about his head. He needed to calm down and play his game, and not overreact to everything. So what if striker was a long shot? The point was to make the team; defending wasn't the end of the world.

"Team Four will kick off," Ian pronounced, placing the ball at Timothy's feet. Backpedalling furiously, he blew his whistle and spun his arm like a windmill. Timothy tapped the ball to John, who gave it straight back to the centre midfielder, who in turn passed promptly to his right. In the face of pressure, the right midfielder relayed it back to Cody. He'd rather have settled into the game before touching the ball, but there it was. He took a few steps to his left, and then heard Timothy bellowing at the top of his lungs as he cut into space toward the sidelines.

It probably made good sense to get on his good side. Cody took one more step and belted the ball left-footed in his direction. Timothy took it in stride and set off downfield. Cody followed slowly, keeping pace with the back line.

"Nice pass," the middle back said to him.

Cody reddened, not quite sure what to say. It was just a pass. No big deal.

Timothy faked inside and took it wide. The defender wasn't fooled and cut him off. Timothy grabbed his shoulder and spun him around. It was such an obvious foul Cody turned to get ready for the free kick. Only there was no whistle. In the clear, Timothy sent a blistering shot to the goalie's right for a goal.

The defender who had been fouled held up his arms and let them flop to his sides.

"Atta boy, Timmer. Play hard, boys. Never give up on a ball," Ian said, looking rather pleased.

Cody felt bad for the defender. He'd played Timothy perfectly.

Team Three kicked off and moved the ball to the left. After a few short passes, the midfielder chipped the ball deep toward the right sideline. Cody raced over and, with a man on his heels, let it bounce once before heading it out of bounds.

A forward ran past and Cody shifted over to mark him, a good thing, too, as the ball was thrown in his direction. The forward tried a spin move to the outside but he hadn't really gotten control of the ball, and Cody poked it away. It rolled over the line for another throw-in. This time, the ball was tossed to a trailing midfielder, and the forward Cody was marking ran into the penalty area.

Timothy and John didn't bother coming back, which gave Team Three plenty of room to pass the ball around. Cody and his fellow defenders shifted left and right as the ball went back and forth between the Team Three forwards and midfielders. Team Four did a good job plugging any holes, though, and the ball remained on the perimeter.

Finally, a midfielder tried to play the ball through the defence. The middle defender was able to get a foot on it, however, and the ball deflected to the right.

Cody corralled the loose ball about fifteen metres from his own goal and headed upfield. The sudden turnover meant he had lots of space.

"Pass it! Hurry!"

Once again Timothy was yelling for the ball. Cody could've continued on the attack but, like before, he figured a pass was the better choice. He was about to deliver the ball when Timothy spun and sprinted between two defenders, looking back over his shoulder. What had been a simple pass was now a killer. Cody would have to loft it over the defenders, but not too far or the goalie would get it — and he had to do it now because a midfielder was closing in.

Cody cut left to give himself a bit of an angle, and then swept his left foot under the ball to give it some extra lift.

"Pathetic," he grunted to himself. Totally left it short.

But Cody's harsh judgment proved premature. As the defender turned to head it away, he stumbled slightly and didn't jump high enough. The ball grazed his head, which actually helped because the ball didn't bounce very much, and Timothy could run onto it without slowing down.

Cody didn't see the end of the play, however. The midfielder crashed into him and they both fell hard to the ground.

The whistle blew. "Awesome goal, Timothy," Ian said gleefully. "Two touches, two goals. You see that, Team Four? Feed your strikers and they won't disappoint."

The midfielder got up without a word and went back to his end. Cody stayed down, his right leg throbbing a bit. What if his leg was really hurt? His mom would go insane and he wouldn't be able to play again until he was eighteen!

"Beauty pass," he heard.

The middle back lent Cody a hand and pulled him to his feet.

"That was your goal all the way," he said.

Cody was still a little preoccupied about his leg. "Um . . . thanks," he managed.

"Not that Timothy would notice," the boy added.

He said it kind of funny, and Cody laughed. It was true. Timothy didn't seem like the type to give anyone else credit.

"Name's William," the defender continued. "Are you sure you're not a defender? You look like you've been on the back line all your life."

Cody flexed his leg a few times. It felt okay, just a little banged up. "I've always been a striker. Don't really know what I'm doing back here, to be honest — hoping not to make a mistake, I guess."

William tossed his head back and laughed. "That's what playing D is all about." He pointed to the other end. "Heads up. They're coming."

Cody shifted to his position.

"Excuse me, son. What's your name?"

Henry was on the sidelines.

"I'm Cody Dorsett, Coach."

"That was a nice play. Good vision, and it was a difficult

pass since Timothy didn't give you much of an angle. In the future, you might consider not making that pass, however. It was low percentage, and if the defender hadn't misplayed it you would've given the ball away."

Cody felt the energy leave his body. Just his luck that the coach would see him make a dumb play; he'd known he shouldn't have passed.

"Don't get down on yourself," Henry added. "You showed some skills there. Very impressive. Keep it up."

That made him feel better. "Thanks, Coach. I will."

Henry nodded in a friendly way. His smile disappeared when Ian ran over.

"Did you check out Timmer? He's already got two goals. Kid's unstoppable, even better than last year."

Henry didn't respond.

"I forgot to tell you that I'm working on another tournament. Very big-time. Lots of scouts will be there. I've even gotten a few feelers about Timothy from some European development clubs. Can you believe it? Europe! Aren't you totally stoked?"

Henry put his hands in his pockets. "That must be exciting for you."

"Let's keep the tournament thing quiet between us boys, okay?" Ian continued. "I've told the other Dragons, obviously, but I don't want it to get out until we pick the team. And don't worry about the budget; I'll cover the cost of the bus. No way we're carpooling like a bunch of losers, right?"

"That seems like something we should talk about at the parents' meeting," Henry said.

Ian slapped him on the back. "I'll put it on the agenda.

Just wanted to give you the heads-up."

Henry left to watch the other game. Ian blew his whistle. "Get it together, Team Three. Timothy's beating you single-handed. C'mon."

It didn't take Team Three long to figure out that Timothy and John were only interested in scoring, and they never passed except to each other. So, as soon as either of them got the ball, three or four Team Three players would surround them, and invariably the ball would be turned over. As a result, Team Three controlled most of the play, and if not for a few spectacular saves by Team Four's goalie, a kid named David, they would have won. When Ian blew his whistle to end the scrimmage, Team Four had managed to hold on for a 2–1 victory.

Cody instinctively reached behind his thigh to feel his leg. Despite Henry's encouragement, Cody had never got comfortable on defence and continued to pass as soon as he got the ball. He wasn't too upset to hear the whistle. After not playing for so long he was really tired and his leg was definitely stiffening. Still, it was awesome to be back on the pitch.

"Coach is going to talk to you boys," Ian bellowed. "Everyone back to centre."

Cody took it slow, stretching out his leg a few times. Most of the players were already back when he sat down to wait for Henry.

Kenneth and Luca sat next to him.

"How'd it go?" Kenneth asked. "Pop any in?"

"I played D," Cody answered "I hardly knew what I was doing."

"Me, too," Kenneth said. He looked terribly disappointed. "They stuck me at left back. All I did was kick it upfield for an hour."

"What about me up front?" Luca demanded. "I told that manager guy, Mitch, when I was born my mom asked the doctor what I was. The doctor said, 'He's a defender.'"

Henry interrupted them. "You all did very well, and I saw a lot of good skills and a lot of hard work."

Ian stepped in front of him, Mitch and the other Dragons with him. "But we have to cut ten to twelve players before the second tryout this Tuesday, so we'll be making the calls tonight and tomorrow," Ian said.

Mitch nodded emphatically.

Henry moved to the side and a pained look crossed his face. He looked even more tired than before the tryout. "Let's finish off with some races," he said. "We'll have all the defenders line up at centre, the midfielders behind them, and then the strikers. I assume the strikers are the fastest, but anyone is welcome to race with them if they want."

The players let out a big cheer. Not Cody, though. He was exhausted and his leg hurt. But he had to show Henry he had striker speed.

Luca did well and came a very respectable second behind William.

"Midfielders next," Ian announced.

"Good luck," Cody said to Kenneth.

Kenneth tilted his head back. "I think I'll chance it with the strikers."

Most of the midfielders finished in a big pack, with one

guy that Cody thought was named Jordan pulling ahead in the last three metres to win it. The strikers were next.

"Show 'em who's boss," Ian called out to Timothy.

"Bear down, John," Mitch sounded.

Cody kicked his right foot into the ground to get a good foothold and readied himself. It would be over if he blew his leg out.

"Go!" Ian screamed.

Cody was halfway down the field before he had the presence of mind to check out the competition — and what a shock when he saw that he was actually first, with Kenneth a couple of steps behind to his left. Chest burning, legs shaking, and teeth clenched, he gutted out the last fifteen metres. He'd won. Immediately, he bent over at the waist and put his hands on his knees, gasping for breath.

Kenneth offered up a high-five. "For a defender you sure move like a striker. I think I got windburn running behind you."

Cody could barely hold up his hand. "Were you in second?" Cody asked.

Kenneth stretched his arms, shoulder height. "Who cares?" he said, and then added, "although I did come in second."

"That was a totally bogus start," Cody heard Timothy complain. "I wasn't even ready. We should have a restart. Those guys took off way before you said 'Go'."

Kenneth elbowed Cody and chuckled.

"I don't think that's necessary," Henry said in a flat voice. "I've seen you play. It's okay."

"It's still unfair," Timothy snorted, and he stomped off to complain to his dad.

Kenneth tugged on Cody's shirt. "I'm glad I don't have to beat him again. I'm tired."

Kenneth didn't look tired at all. As for himself, Cody felt as if he could've fallen asleep right then and there.

"So I'll see you on Tuesday," Kenneth said, as Luca joined them.

Cody was confused. How did he know who made the cut? "I think the coaches are going to call us, or something . . ."

Kenneth laughed. "We'll make it. We're the speed demons. Besides, you and I got all the personality — unlike him," he said, poking Luca in the chest.

"I got something way better," Luca said.

"Like what?"

"I don't pee in my bed anymore."

Kenneth burst out laughing. "Okay, you win," he said.

For a moment all three boys were silent.

"So . . . We'll see ya," Kenneth said to Cody.

"Sure . . . I mean . . . I hope to see you guys, too," he stammered.

That couldn't have sounded lamer if he tried. Great time for a mind freeze. Cody waved at the two boys as they left the pitch, and then he headed to the parking lot to find his dad. His leg was sore after the race, but he didn't want the coach, or his dad, to see him limp. So, he forced himself to walk normally.

His dad came out of the car to meet him. "How was the tryout?" he asked.

"Didn't you see it?"

"Of course I did," he said. "You were great — just great. I wondered what you thought."

Classic dad. He probably worked the whole time. He must be the only kid in the world whose dad hated sports.

"It was okay," Cody said, as they got into the car. "They'll call us tonight or tomorrow about the next tryout."

"Wonderful. Let's get back before your mom worries."

Cody jammed his skullcap on. During the entire ride home a single question occupied his mind.

Would he make the cut?

Cody pawed at the ground with his cleats. The thrill of getting asked to the second tryout was wearing off quickly as he listencd to Henry and Ian argue about drills. Twice already, Ian and Mitch had run onto the pitch and ordered Henry to change something. The three other Dragons also came onto the pitch to offer tips to their sons. The last twenty minutes had been spent practising set pieces, with Timothy taking all the kicks, and then it was on to penalties. The only good thing was that Cody scored on his two shots. He'd used his left foot and had been worried about messing up, so he was happy about that.

More unsettling to Cody was that his mom had decided to come. He'd tried every trick in the book: tryouts were boring, it might be late, he didn't know how much he'd play, she could come to a game if he made the team.

She wouldn't listen, and there she was on the sidelines; he could feel her eyes following his every move, which made it harder to focus. Someone had clapped after he scored on the penalty shots and he could only hope it hadn't been his mom — even though he knew it had.

"Okay, so just run the drill. We've got lots of notes to go over," Ian said.

"Listen up, boys," Henry said, looking as tired as ever. "We don't have much time left, so let's have the defenders in the penalty area and the strikers and midfielders at midfield."

Cody lined up with the strikers. Timothy stepped in front.

"Behind me, dudes," he said.

Cody didn't say anything, and neither did anyone else.

"We're gonna do one-on-ones," Henry said. "Show me your best moves and try to score. Defenders will try to stop you." He motioned for David to go into the net. "Are you ready?"

David waved, and Henry blew his whistle. Timothy took off, dribbling hard to his right, Luca defending. Cody hoped Luca did well. He was tired of the Timothy Show.

"Cut him off early," he muttered under his breath, and, weirdly, Luca did exactly that, charging forward from the box to challenge. Timothy reacted by chipping the ball outside, but Luca was ready and stuck out his left foot to knock the ball away. Timothy didn't stop, and they collided.

Timothy got the worst of it and flopped to the pitch. "Foul," he yelled.

Luca grinned and went back to the defenders. Timothy wasn't so ready to give it up, however. "How's that not interference?" he said angrily to Henry.

The coach gestured to the other strikers. "It's okay," he said. "Why don't you just rejoin the line."

"Call it, next time," Timothy shot back. "No point letting it go. Ref will call it in the game. The dude thinks it's hockey."

Henry blew his whistle. "Next up," he said quietly.

Timothy threw his hands in the air. Ian and Mitch were back on the pitch.

"You really gotta call fouls," Ian said to Henry. "I know how tough it is to stop Timothy without fouling, but if kids learn bad habits . . ."

Henry walked away.

The next player cut wide left and let loose a long shot from outside the penalty area. David handled it easily, rolling the ball to Henry in one motion. Cody was totally impressed by David's coolness under pressure and his athleticism. Cody wondered if he'd played on the team last year.

When Cody's turn came a boy named Antonio stepped forward to defend. His dad was a Dragon. The whistle blew.

"All yours, Toni," his dad said.

"Egg-Head's got nothin'. Shut him down," John said, loudly enough for Cody to hear.

Cody pushed forward.

"You got my ball," Antonio taunted. He approached quickly, crouching low, his left foot ahead slightly.

Cody had noticed in the races last tryout that Antonio,

while a big guy, wasn't exactly the fastest player on the pitch. He slowed to let him get closer, and then, when Antonio was about three metres away, Cody faked a step-over and chipped the ball to the left with his outside left foot. Off-footed, Antonio turned too slowly, and Cody raced past him and stormed in on goal.

David came way out, arms wide apart, bent forward at the waist. Cody knew he had to be decisive because David was an aggressive goalie and he'd try to force him early. He slid to his left, took a few more steps to get closer to the net, and then struck the ball with his left foot, sending the ball across the goal to the far side about two metres off the ground.

The misdirection shot fooled David, but he was so good that he was able to get his left hand on the ball. He slowed it down, but not enough to stop the bouncing ball from nicking the inside of the post and going in.

Cody was totally stoked. That might get Henry's attention.

"Cheap move, Chicken-Leg," Antonio said to him as he passed. "Next time I'm gonna actually try."

Cody pretended he hadn't heard the dis.

Like it was his fault his right leg was skinny! And he wasn't gonna tell anyone about it, either. None of their business!

Cody barely watched the other players while he waited for his next turn. And, sure enough, when it came, Antonio was defending. Unlike last time, Antonio came out slowly, a determined look on his face.

Antonio had assumed a fairly wide stance, which gave

Cody an idea. He set off at a fast pace, dribbling with his right foot, and when he got close he slipped the ball between the big defender's feet. Antonio spun, but Cody got to it first. Antonio decided to try a slide tackle with his right leg. Cody anticipated the desperation move and kicked the ball ahead. Antonio missed completely, and once again Cody was in alone.

David charged the ball. He underestimated Cody's speed, however. A shot of pain flared up into Cody's hip as he raced to get there first. It was worth it, though. Cody nicked the ball on and it slid past David's outstretched left foot and into the open net.

Cody allowed himself a smile; in a bizarre way, the pain felt good.

What didn't feel good was Antonio's knee driving into his right leg and his shoulder smashing into Cody's shoulder, knocking him clear off his feet. Cody lay on the ground clutching his leg. It felt as if a red-hot iron had burned him, like his thigh was on fire.

He dimly heard Luca saying, "What are you — a goof or something?"

"What's your problem? I ran into him. Get lost," Antonio shot back.

"You did that on purpose," Kenneth said.

"Forget you."

Eyes closed tightly, light-headed, and almost sick to his stomach, Cody forced himself to focus on breathing and to isolate the pain to one spot, a trick Dr. Charya had taught him to handle the cancer treatments. As usual, it worked pretty well, and after a few deep breaths the pain began to go away, and he could open his eyes.

The first person he saw made him want to close his eyes again. His mom was on one knee and she began to rub the small of his back.

"Honey, it's me. You'll be okay. Just try to keep calm. The ambulance should be here soon."

He heard a few kids giggle off to the side. "Egg-Head's a mama's boy," one of them said, and the laughter got louder.

"Try not to move your leg," she said in a quivering voice.

Cody rolled onto his back and brought his knees to his chest. He wished the ground would swallow him up.

"Please don't move, dear," she said, pushing his legs back to the ground. "Let's wait for the ambulance. I don't want to risk making things worse."

"I'll be fine," he whispered fiercely. He looked over and saw Timothy, John, and Antonio grinning like idiots. Another guy was saying something in Timothy's ear that made him laugh hysterically.

"How is he?" Henry asked gently.

"Do you allow that kind of behaviour on your team?" his mom said loudly. "That was a deliberate attempt to injure."

Cody gritted his teeth and forced himself onto his knees. He was too angry at his mom to care about the pain.

"I didn't see it, Ma'am. I'm sorry. I was talking to Ian," Henry explained.

"Soccer can be a tough sport," Ian said.

"Yes, a very tough sport," Mitch said.

"He should be okay," Antonio's dad said.

"Stay down," his mom said to him as he struggled to his feet.

"You better stay down. You'll hurt yourself," Timothy said in a high voice.

"Sometimes kids collide," Ian continued. "It happens. Your son's probably not used to how hard these boys play. This might be a tougher brand of soccer than he's used to . . ."

"I'll let you know that my son has had . . . my son has a serious . . ." His mom paused.

She was going to say it. This was the worst moment of his life.

"My son was . . . top scorer on his team; and he's used to playing hard," she said, almost in a whisper.

Ian cleared his throat. "Yes. Well. Maybe your son should take a break on the sidelines. Your son's name is . . .?"

"His name is Cody Dorsett," she said.

"Yes, of course. Your son is a fine player." Ian clapped his hands a few times and in a loud voice said, "Let's get back in line and keep going with the drill."

"I think practice has been long enough," Henry said slowly.

"Okay. Certainly," Ian said. "Just to let everyone know, we'll be making our assessments tonight. We already have twelve commitments and we would like to start the season with seventeen players, which will leave us a spot to fill from someone cut from the Premier division."

"Thanks everyone for coming out," Henry said. "You're all fine players, and I wish you all the best even if it turns out we can't make an offer. I've made lots of mistakes in my time, so please don't be upset if you don't get asked. As far as I'm concerned, you all have the talent to play at this level."

Ian squinted and with a shrug added, "But we've got a solid handle on the talent and only the very best will get an offer."

The players began to drift off the pitch.

"Can you walk or should we wait for a stretcher?" Cody's mom said to him.

His leg would have to fall off before he'd let the guys see him taken off on a stretcher. He set out for the sidelines, pain shooting up the side of his leg with each step. No matter how hard he tried he couldn't keep from limping.

"Let me help, honey," his mom said, and she tried to put her arm around his waist.

Cody moved away. Was she gonna put diapers on him next?

"Hey, Cody. Are you alright?"

Kenneth and Luca came over. They both looked really serious.

"I'm fine . . . no problem. A bit of a charley horse, is all. It's nothing."

Kenneth nodded a few times. "Good. That was a total cheap shot."

"The boy was just mad you smoked him twice," Luca said.

Cody suddenly realized he wouldn't see these guys again. Even though he barely knew them, for some reason he kinda thought they were friends, at least the closest things to friends he had in this place.

"See ya," he managed, and he limped away as fast as he could. *Egg-Head the mama's boy. That's what they were thinking.*

His mom caught up with him. "Cody, that was rude of you," his mom said. "Those boys were asking how you were and you just . . ."

It was on the tip of his tongue to say "Shut up, Mom, and thanks for ruining everything!" But he didn't. She'd get all upset and say, "Sorry that I love you so much" and other stuff like that, and it would become a huge deal. He just wanted to get in the car and go.

"Excuse me, Cody."

Henry jogged slowly toward them. For the first time he noticed the coach had a bad right knee. It was painful to watch him run, as if one hip was way higher than the other.

"You did well today," he said, slightly out of breath. He was smiling, though. "I wanted to tell you that. You have good instincts and you're probably the fastest boy on the pitch."

Cody was overwhelmed.

"Thanks very much, Coach," his mom answered. "I know I'm biased, but I think he's a terrific player." She laughed.

"Henry, can you come over here?" Ian called out. He and the Dragons were huddled around his clipboard.

"Ice that leg to take the swelling down, and then treat it with heat tomorrow," Henry said. The smile was gone. "Take care, Cody." He turned and walked over to Ian and the others.

Cody headed toward the car.

"Honey, we have to wait for the ambulance."

He slapped the side of his head and groaned. "You didn't really call an ambulance, did you?"

"I'm sorry, honey." She laughed nervously. "I guess I sort of panicked a little. I thought your leg was broken." She brushed her hair from her face. "Still, you can barely put any weight on it, and it's not worth the risk. Let's just sit over on that bench until . . ."

"No," he exploded. "You're so . . . I don't need an ambulance because I bumped into someone. Rush me to the hospital the next time I stub my toe, why don't you?"

Before his shocked mom could answer a fire truck rolled into the parking lot, siren blaring. Two firemen jumped out.

"I'm sorry, Cody," his mom said. "But I think you now understand why it's too soon for you to play soccer. We need to slow down and wait for your leg to recover its strength. When I hurt my knee at university I had to take six months off and . . . Cody, are you listening?"

The two firemen were carrying a big, red metal box.

Cody tossed the magazine on the table. It slid onto the floor. He ignored it and slumped down in his chair. They'd been waiting for the doctor forever, and his butt was killing him; he was so bored he thought he might seriously lose his mind.

"Honey, I know it's taking a long time, but I asked you before to stop fidgeting. You're doing a good job; I just need a little better behaviour," his mom said.

"I'm not five years old," he said. "You talk to me like I still watch *Dora the Explorer*."

She gave him a stern look. "Then don't act like you do — and keep the ice on your leg."

"My leg is frozen solid. I've been icing it for ten hours."

"I don't think we've been here that long."

"Feels like it."

She sighed, got up, and went to the reception desk. "Is there any way that Dr. Charya can see us? All we need is ten minutes, and we've been here for two hours."

The receptionist pushed her glasses firmly into place. "She is extremely busy, and you didn't have an appointment. When I have a chance, I'll fit you in." She looked over at Cody. "Like I said, I don't think this is an emergency, and it would be best if we scheduled a visit for another day."

"Excuse me, but my son had major surgery on his right thigh less than six months ago, and he suffered a severe trauma to the same area today. He can barely walk. So I'm not sure I agree with your expert opinion. Perhaps we should let Dr. Charya decide."

His mom was using her pretend polite voice.

"Have you told Dr. Charya that we're here?" his mom continued.

"She knows," the receptionist replied.

"Then perhaps you could remind her," his mom said.

"If you could just have a seat in the reception area, she shouldn't be too much longer."

"That's what you said an hour ago, and then thirty minutes ago, and then ten minutes ago."

The receptionist took off her glasses and rubbed her eyes with her fingers. She picked up the phone, said a few words that Cody couldn't hear, and then put the receiver down.

"She'll see you now," she said blankly, and then began pounding away on her keyboard.

"Come on, dear. Do you need help?" his mom asked.

"No."

Dr. Charya gave him a big smile when he walked in. He really liked her and he smiled back in spite of his dark mood. Even when his parents, especially his mom, were losing it during his treatments, Dr. Charya always stayed calm; she taught had him tons of stuff, like the breathing trick, so the treatments didn't hurt so much, and she answered his questions so he understood what was happening.

"How is my Cody doing?" she asked. For such a small person her voice was really loud.

"Not so good," his mom answered. "He was playing soccer, which I'll never forgive myself for, and another boy ran into him, into his leg, a terrible blow, and he fell to the ground and couldn't move for . . . I don't exactly remember . . . maybe five minutes."

"It wasn't close to that long," Cody said. "More like thirty seconds."

"What happened?" the doctor asked, quietly this time.

They both began to answer. Dr. Charya held up her hands. "How about Cody tells me, first."

His mom frowned and folded her arms.

"I was playing soccer — it was a tryout — and a guy ran into me and gave me a charley horse," Cody said.

"Allow the doctor to examine you before you make a diagnosis," his mom said. "Please tell him, Dr. Charya, how important it is to be careful with his leg."

Cody threw up his hands. "Please tell her you don't get cancer from soccer, and it's just a charley horse, and she totally freaked out and ran onto the pitch and made me look like a total loser."

His mom's eyes opened wide. "Again, I'm sorry for running onto the pitch. I know that was wrong and I know it was embarrassing for you. But when I saw you writhing in pain . . ." Her voice began to crack.

"How about I take a look at that leg, and then we can discuss things," Dr. Charya said. "Hop up on the table."

She poked and prodded his leg, mostly around the incision site, and after a minute or so turned to his mom.

"Cheryl, you've been through a terribly stressful time. I have two kids myself and can only imagine how you've suffered. As I've told you before, I admire your dedication to Cody's health, and I know you'd do anything to help him. But the surgery was very successful, and so was the chemotherapy. I see no reason to worry. The chance of the cancer returning is low. He has a bad bruise — in other words, a charley horse. Give it some ice, switch to heat tomorrow, and he'll be good in a day or two. He's young."

Cody glared in triumph at his mom. Dr. Charya put her hand on his shoulder.

"And maybe you could be a bit nicer to your mom and appreciate how much she loves you and worries about you, and maybe be a bit more patient, too," she said to him. "That's not always easy for a thirteen-year-old boy, but could you?"

Cody suddenly felt bad. "I'm sorry, Mom," he blurted.

She was crying. "I know I overreacted," she said. "I would've been angry at my mom if she'd run onto the soccer pitch when I was playing. But, Doctor, please tell Cody why it's such a bad idea for him to play soccer."

The doctor looked puzzled. "What's wrong with him playing soccer?"

His mom looked shocked. "Tell him about getting hurt, and how his leg could be severely damaged in the long term, and how he has lost a lot of muscle, and soccer is too hard on the legs, and . . ."

"Cheryl, if his leg can't take the strain, then by all means he should delay playing sports again. I don't think that's the case, however. The tumour was localized, and I took great care not to damage the muscle." She smiled at Cody. "He looks healthy and strong to me."

"Dr. Charya, wouldn't it be better if he played next year?"

She shook her head. "I understand your concern, but there is no medical reason to wait. Frankly, sports are the best way to build his leg back up." She eyed him closely. "Are you doing your exercises?"

"Every morning and night," he said eagerly.

"And icing it — and taking the Epsom-salt baths?"

"Totally. I stretch twice a day and ice it after; and I take a bath at night."

"That's great. It'll make a big difference, especially after you play soccer."

Dr. Charya laughed and ruffled his head with her hand, and then turned to his mom. "There are other reasons for him to play, too. It's what he loves to do, and this is the time for things to get back to normal. And in this case, Cheryl, normal means parents driving kids around like crazy people to practices and games and tournaments, and dealing with the ten thousand other things our kids get into."

His mom sighed. "Okay. I get it. I need to lighten up. I just got so scared when he didn't get up. Sorry for bothering you."

"Don't be silly. I'm sorry for the wait. Sometimes my staff is a bit overprotective of my time. You come whenever you have a concern."

"I appreciate that."

The doctor smiled brightly and patted Cody's arm. "I've got a few more patients, so if you'll excuse me I have someone waiting in another examining room."

Cody hopped off the table when she left — a bad move as a shot of pain ran down his leg. Luckily, his mom didn't notice him flinch.

"We should get back. Your dad will be worried. I left a message on his cell that we were at the hospital," she said.

Cody struggled to appear calm as they walked back to the reception area. He walked through the doors and stopped short. "Hey, Dad! What're you doing here?"

In a serious tone, his dad answered, "I'm here because my son is in the hospital and there's a problem with his leg."

Cody got the feeling he was speaking to his mom, not him.

"Dr. Cherry said I was fine," Cody said. Calling her Dr. Cherry was a private joke between them, on account of her name and the fact that she always had red cheeks.

"I got worried when Cody got hit in the leg at the tryouts," his mom began.

"That's not how you made it sound on the phone," his dad said.

"I have a charley horse," Cody interjected. "A guy ran into me on a one-on-one drill."

His dad looked at his mom.

She pursed her lips. "Perhaps I shouldn't have called an ambulance. I'm sorry."

His dad's shoulders slumped before he got up. "It's okay. At least we know there's no problem," he said. All of a sudden he brightened up. "I can't believe I almost forgot," he exclaimed. "Your coach called me when I was coming over here."

Cody felt his heart begin to beat extra fast.

"You made it! You're officially a member of the Lions. The coach said some very nice things about you. He told me he insisted that you be added to the roster. He asked if you were okay, too."

"What did you say," Cody managed.

"I told him that I hadn't seen you yet, but that you were at the hospital, and . . ."

"No! About the team?"

He laughed. "I said I'd ask but that there was a ninety-nine point nine nine nine per cent chance you'd say yes."

"Call him back quick before he gives my spot to someone else," Cody said.

His dad laughed even harder. "I arranged to call him tomorrow morning. Don't worry — you're on the team."

Cody gave him a hug.

As if on cue, they both turned to look at his mom. She held her hands up over her head.

"I surrender. I admit I'm not thrilled with you playing, but the doctor said you could, so . . ."

"When do practices start?" Cody asked his dad.

"Apparently, the manager is going to email the schedule," his dad said.

"We should get going," his mom said. "It's getting late, and Cody needs to get to bed."

He followed his parents down the hall to the elevators, and when other people got on he turned to the wall so they wouldn't see the ridiculous grin on his face.

He was gonna play soccer this summer!

The months of hospital visits and treatments were over.

It was like a dream.

The elevator doors opened slowly. It was sure nice to leave. He really hated this place.

7

Cody's stomach growled and he twisted his body toward the car window. "I'm starving," he said.

"I told you to eat before practice," his mom said angrily. "We're at the pitch already . . . I could run to a corner store and get a chocolate bar or an energy drink . . . or . . ."

"I'm only kidding," he said. The thought of her coming onto the pitch to feed him was way worse than a little hunger.

She sighed. "Cody, you'll seriously be the death of me one day." She turned the radio off. "Are you nervous about the first practice?" she asked without warning.

"Nah. Not really. Maybe a bit about how my leg will feel. It still hurts from the charley horse."

To be honest he was actually very, very nervous. He didn't know anyone. The Egg-Head thing was definitely not good; that kind of thing could stick, and he couldn't play with his skullcap on. That would look even weirder.

"Did you do your stretching exercises and take your bath with the Epsom salts and ice your leg?"

"Yes, Mom."

"Make sure you tell your coach you're a striker," she said, as they pulled into the parking lot.

"Okay. I will."

That was one thing he wasn't going to do!

"And don't run too hard right away; let your leg get loose. And if you get too tired you can always . . ."

"I'm fine, Mom," he snapped. "It's just a practice." He closed the door and ran off to the pitch.

A bunch of players had formed a big circle at midfield. They were waiting for Henry, Mitch, and Ian to stop talking.

"Hey, Cody. How's it going?" Kenneth said to him.

Cody sat next to him. "I'm good." Luca waved, a big grin on his face. Cody noticed a few players staring at him, and John put his hand over his forehead and pulled back his hair, which made Timothy and Antonio break up.

"I was hoping you'd make it," Kenneth said.

"I knew you two would," Cody said. He was overjoyed to see them.

"How's the leg?" Luca asked.

He felt himself blush. No need to be reminded of that. "It's fine," he said quickly. "Just a charley horse."

"Let's get into a groin stretch," Henry said.

"Why don't we just get started," Ian said, clapping his hand against his clipboard. "You get better by playing soccer, not sittin' around, right, boys?"

No one answered.

"Real lame, Dad," Timothy said.

Ian waved him off. "Coach is gonna explain our basic formation, and then ..." He held up his clipboard and with raised eyebrows said, "I'll read out the starting eleven."

Cody's nerves kicked into high gear. Sure it was crazy to think he'd start, but the coach had told his dad that he liked him. So, maybe ...?

Henry cleared his voice, but before he could speak Ian cut in.

"First off, I have an announcement," Ian said, a sly grin crossing his face. "The boys here," and he motioned to the Dragons, "have come up with something special that I think you're gonna like. How does a trip to Florida for a tournament sound?"

"Awesome," John said, and he high-fived with Antonio.

"I knew about it, guys, but was sworn to secrecy," Timothy said.

Cody noticed that the Dragons had new hats and shirts.

Ian kept talking. "We'll have a bus so we can go in style, and I've booked a hotel with a pool, and we'll probably end up playing about seven games to get to the finals. It's one of the biggest tournaments in North America, like, number three or four or ... not sure of the number. Anyway, it'll be totally intense and cool and ... we're gonna trash every side we play. Right, boys?"

This time they all cheered.

Henry rested a whiteboard against his hip and drew a formation with a black marker. Cody instantly recognized it as the 4-4-2.

"Maybe we can focus a bit on soccer, now," Henry said.

"We won't be trashing anyone without a whole lot of hard work."

Ian stepped in front of the board. "The key to making this work is getting the ball to our strikers at pace, and then having the outside midfielders support." He took a marker from his pocket. "Can I have that for a sec?" he asked Henry.

"You need to get your own whiteboard," Henry said, before handing it over.

"Good idea. Mitch, we should pick up a couple," Ian said.

Mitch wrote on his clipboard. Ian began to draw a bunch of arrows on Henry's diagram.

The more Ian spoke the less Cody understood. Why didn't Henry do the coaching?

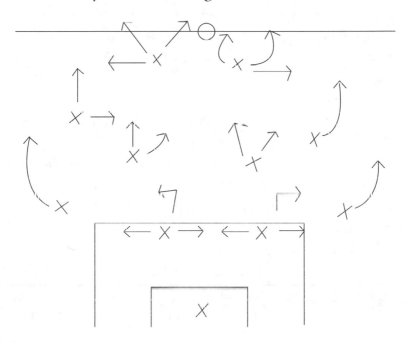

"So, Henry, why don't we have the boys run through a few plays?" Ian said.

Henry merely nodded.

Ian slapped his forehead. "I forgot — the starters. Now where is that piece of paper?" He made a big show of looking around before pulling it from his binder with a flourish. Kenneth smirked and rolled his eyes.

"We don't have to do this now," Henry said.

"Nonsense," Ian replied. "But before I read it out, everyone should understand we had a lot of returning players, so new kids shouldn't feel disappointed. It's a long season, and everyone will play a little bit. Now, please stand up when your name's called."

"So lame, Dad," Timothy chirped.

"In goal, we have David. We might pick up another goalie; not sure yet," Ian continued. "The defenders are William, Nathan, Antonio, and Michael. Our midfield this year is Austin, Tyler, Jordan, and Brandon. And our strikers," he winked as if they were all in on the joke, "will be John and Timothy."

"All those guys were from last year's team, except for David," Luca told Cody and Kenneth.

"We had an awesome last season, and we led the league in goals," Ian said. "With David in net, we should be a lock for the championship," He looked very pleased with that thought.

"No one's got our talent," Mitch said.

"Starting eleven down at the far end," Ian declared. "Let's get this party started."

The starters wandered to their side, with Henry shuffling

slowly behind. Ian and Mitch left abruptly, leaving the six subs in the middle of the pitch.

Kenneth broke the silence. "My name is Kenneth and my hobby this year will be watching soccer."

Luca piped up next. "I'm Luca, and my hobby will be watching Kenneth watch soccer."

Kenneth nudged a kid next to him. "Introduce yourself, bro."

"I'm Anthony," he growled.

He didn't seem too happy.

Kenneth didn't appear to notice. "Me and Anth played midfield together last season. I believe soccer is called the Beautiful Game because of the way we played." He nudged Anthony again. "Ain't you gonna watch me?"

Anthony kicked at the grass with his spikes. "I wanna play. This is a joke. The best players should start. That Austin kid doesn't deserve a spot — no way."

Cody found his outburst a bit awkward, and he guessed the others did as well since no one agreed or said anything. Kenneth alone was unfazed.

"Let's continue, shall we? So who are you?" he said to Cody.

All eyes shifted to him. "Well, I'm Cody. I didn't play last season. Moved here from . " He was babbling, and no one cared. Why didn't he just say his name? "I'll watch you, Kenneth . . . and you too, Luca," he said in a rush.

To his surprise Kenneth and Luca burst out laughing. "We're gonna have a super old time, a-watching and a-singin' away the entire season," Kenneth said gleefully.

"Ain't that the truth," Luca giggled.

"It'll be just super . . . 'cause we are . . . the Super Subs . . . that's why. I like it. Who needs the Starting Eleven? I wanna be a Super Sub. Now, who are the last of the Super Subs?"

The other boys introduced themselves. One kid was named Ryan, a midfielder, and the other was Jacob, a defender like Luca. Cody remembered playing against Ryan in the first scrimmage. He was a pretty good player, if memory served; Jacob had also impressed him at the tryouts.

A whistle blew. "How about you boys spread out across the pitch and play some defence," Henry said to the newly named Super Subs. "We're going to pass the ball around and work out a few plays. I know you're outnumbered, but do your best."

"We're on it, Coach," Kenneth enthused, jumping to his feet. "Let's get 'em, Super Subs."

"You've lost it," Anthony said. He walked off.

"Tell me something I don't know," Kenneth joked. He elbowed Cody. "You're the only striker, so why don't you play up. We'll play a 1-3-2, with Luca and Jacob at the back. Cool?"

Cody nodded, and it was cool. Kenneth and Luca were a riot and it would be fun to watch the games with them. Jacob and Ryan seemed nice, too. Anthony — not so much. Still, the Starting Eleven couldn't play all the time. Henry had to make some substitutions. At least he was a Super Sub, and that beat sitting at home anytime.

Tyler took the ball and pressed up the left side. Cody cut over to head him off, the disappointment of not starting forgotten in the sheer joy of playing soccer again.

The United midfielder chipped the ball into the box, perfectly timed for a hard charging striker to launch himself at the ball and head it toward the top right corner. David threw himself to his left and managed to get a fist on it. The ball grazed the crossbar and bounced out of play.

The Dragons let out a collective sigh of relief.

"Awesome save, David."

"Come on, Lions. Let's get it outta our end."

"Control the ball. Hard on it."

Most of the other Lions' parents were standing or sitting in chairs closer to midfield. For the most part they'd been quiet. Cody couldn't blame them. Not much had happened to cheer about. The Lions had barely touched the ball, and now, deep in the second half, the score was 5 0. Cody wasn't enjoying himself too much, either. At first, it had been fun to listen to Kenneth's jokes and feel part of the team, even as a Super Sub, but as the game wore on it became pathetically obvious that the Lions didn't have a chance.

"We should pack some snacks," Kenneth said to Luca. "I mean, what was I thinking? How awesome would an ice-cream sundae be right about now?"

"Did you say chocolate sauce on that?" Luca said.

"Like I'd forget the sauce!"

The score didn't seem to bother these two. It was killing Cody. United owned the ball, and he had to admire the way they passed it around and got everyone involved with lots of support. As for the Lions . . . well . . . some guys hustled, like William, and he liked Jordan and Brandon in the midfield. The offence had done nothing all game, however. Every time Timothy got the ball he tried to score by himself.

That hadn't gone well.

As if on cue, Jordan made a neat pass to John at midfield, and Timothy came barrelling over demanding the ball. John passed it square to him.

"I bet Timmer gives it back to John and the defender picks it off," Luca said.

"I bet Timmer keeps it and loses it outside the box," Kenneth countered.

They'd been making bets all game. Cody figured Kenneth would win this one. Timothy hadn't made a pass yet.

And Kenneth was right. Timothy cut inside and tried to split the back line. A United defender swept across and stripped him of the ball. He was a big kid, with long, black hair that hung below his shoulders, and he played hard. He was really good, too. He'd been schooling Timothy all game, and he wasn't afraid of anyone because he and Timothy had been trash-talking and he never backed down.

The defender trapped the ball with his right foot, rocked back, and snapped a line drive to a waiting teammate.

Cody admired the play, and it didn't escape Kenneth's notice, either.

"That guy is like a wall," Kenneth declared.

"I played against him three or four years ago in house league," Luca said. "I think his name is Marco."

"We haven't come close to beating him," Kenneth said.

"I'd like the chance," Anthony said bitterly. "The game is lost, and our useless coach still won't sub us in. Great Starting Eleven."

"Maybe being a Super Sub isn't as awesome as I'd thought," Kenneth said.

"Yeah, maybe," Anthony replied.

"Check out the WWF action, boys," Luca said excitedly.

Timothy was lying on his back, and John was yelling at Marco, who pushed him away with both hands. The referee blew his whistle a few times and came running over.

"Did anyone see what happened?" Kenneth asked.

Cody had, but he was still shy around this group. When no one answered he finally piped up. "After the United defender, that Marco guy, kicked the ball, Timothy gave him an elbow in the back, and then Marco whacked Timothy in the chest with his forearm and sent him down."

"Can't believe I missed Timothy getting his butt kicked," Kenneth said, slapping the ground with his hand. "I'm such a loser. What's the point of being a Super Sub if you don't see that?"

The referee separated John and Marco, and pushed them both toward the sidelines, which allowed Cody and his fellow Super Subs to listen in.

"I'm this close to giving you each red cards," the referee said. "This game is not going to get out of control. Hear me? Do you?"

The players nodded. Cody thought that Marco was trying not to laugh. He sure didn't seem worried.

"Lucky for you I didn't see anything. I have a feeling someone should be kicked out of the game, though," the referee continued.

"It should be him," John said. "He punched Timothy. Do you think he fell to the ground by accident?"

"That's enough," the referee said to him, "or you'll be the one with the red card."

"Why isn't he red-carded? He hit me," Timothy fumed, pointing at Marco.

"No more from you, either," the referee said.

"Get your glasses, ref and make a call; I've been fouled ten times this game. How did you miss him giving me a forearm shiver? Are you stupid?" Timothy stomped his foot on the ground.

The referee turned to Timothy, reached into his shirt pocket, and pulled out a red card.

"You're kidding me," Timothy screamed.

"What game are you watching?" Ian yelled. He'd come

onto the pitch and stood next to his son. "He gets decked and you give him the red card? You're useless."

The rest of the Dragons began heaping more abuse on the referee. Mitch threw his clipboard to the ground. Ian put his arm around Timothy's shoulders as they marched off the pitch. "Can't beat the refs and the other team," he said. "Good work. They were fouling you every time you touched the ball."

"Bogus game," Timothy declared.

Cody felt a finger poke him in the shoulder.

"There's only five minutes, and I don't want John getting a red card. Go on for him at forward. Tell the other players I want to play a 4-4-1. Hopefully, we can keep them from scoring again," Henry said.

Cody was too surprised to say anything. He began to pull off his track pants.

"Why sub now?" Mitch hissed to Henry. "We're down our best striker and we need to keep John out there."

"I thought I'd give Cody a chance to . . ." Henry tried to explain.

"Hey, Ian," Mitch called out. "Henry's taking John off."

Ian came over. "This ain't house league," he snapped. "We're actually trying to win."

Henry ran a hand through his head and let out a long breath.

"The Lions don't throw in the towel," Ian said. "John's our only hope to mount any kind of attack."

Kenneth leaned over to Cody. "Go for it before Henry changes his mind. It's been a dream of mine since I was a little kid to see a Super Sub in a game."

"Maybe I should wait," Cody offered.

"Do it for us," Luca said.

"You may as well," Ryan added.

Cody was torn. If he ran onto the pitch Ian and Mitch would be angry; if he waited the Super Subs would think he was a wuss.

But Henry had told him to play, and he was the coach. Cody headed out.

"Your hat," Luca called to him. Cody scurried back and tossed it to the sidelines.

"Six quick goals and we win," Kenneth said.

Cody laughed as he ran over to John who, with hands on his hips, was staring at the referee.

"What's so funny?" John said to him.

"Nothing. I wasn't laughing at . . ." He stopped himself. "Coach wants a substitution . . . like . . . he wants me to sub for you."

John's mouth gaped open. "This team's a joke," he said, whirling around and storming to the sidelines.

Cody watched him go. The Dragons were giving Henry grief. Kenneth caught his eye and gave him a thumbs-up. Further down the sidelines he spotted his mom. She waved with both hands.

This is what he'd wanted — a chance to play. He bent over to touch his toes and immediately felt the tightness in the back of his right leg. Would he be able to play? Would his leg stand up in a real game?

Or would he totally mess up?

The Lions were huddled about ten metres from the penalty area. Most of his teammates looked less than pleased when he joined them. Antonio made a big show of rolling his eyes and muttering something about "not trying to win anymore."

"I guess it's the B team," Tyler said.

"Let's just get one goal," David said in an urgent tone. Cody knew from practice that David was totally competitive. Giving up five goals had to be brutal for him.

"Henry wants us to play a 4-4-1," Cody said to the group.

"And where will you play?" Antonio sneered.

Cody felt his nerves kick in. "I'm supposed to . . . I'm the . . ."

"Great. The guy doesn't even know his position," Tyler said.

"I know where . . ." he began.

"A dumb Egg-Head," he heard Antonio say to someone.

"Chicken-Leg to the rescue," Tyler said.

Cody stared at their blank faces. He was rooted in place, terrified to say anything and desperate to leave. Then, out of nowhere, David came to his rescue.

"He came on for John. He's the striker. How about we get possession for once?" David said.

The Lions drifted to their positions. The referee's whistle blasted. "United free kick at the spot of the initial foul," he said, jogging to where Timothy and Marco had their scuffle.

That set the Dragons off again.

"How can you give them the free kick? Wake up, ref."

"The fix is obviously on."

"Worst reffing job I've seen in my life."

Marco lofted the ball to the right flank where a winger brought it under control with his chest. A quick pass to the inside support, followed by a pass to space for a breaking forward, and United was on the attack — again. Antonio was caught napping, and it looked like another sure goal until Michael cut in from the outside and, sliding hard, knocked the ball back to David. The alert goalie powered it hard upfield from near the top of the box.

"Come on, Cody. Make us proud," Kenneth hollered.

David's kick was coming right at him, high and hard. He readied himself and jumped, planning to head it to Austin, who was ten metres back. A United defender ruined those plans by pulling down on his shoulder, and the ball skidded off the top of Cody's head and bounced out of bounds.

A United defender grabbed the ball and began the motion for a throw-in. The referee's whistle sounded. He held a yellow card over his head and was running over to the defender.

"What for?" the defender complained.

"Don't give me that. I saw you grab him. No more of that, please."

The defender bowed his head, but Cody caught him sneaking a grin to Marco, who was laughing.

"Free kick, Lions," the referee pronounced.

"Hooray, Super Subs. Way to go up for it," Kenneth howled.

Cody felt better having drawn the foul. Maybe now they'd ease up on the Egg-Head garbage. He stationed himself even with the United back line. Tyler and Brandon came up from midfield. Two United defenders marked them. Nobody paid much attention to him, however. Jordan took the ball from the ref for the kick. Cody doubted he'd kick it to him, but he readied himself all the same. He prided himself on his headers, and always loved a chance to go up for the ball.

Jordan wasted no time. He took two steps forward and punched it up the middle, fairly hard, and without much loft, about three metres to Cody's right. Out of the corner of his eye he saw Marco move onto the ball. Cody took two steps and jumped, straining desperately to flick it in Tyler's direction.

The ball hit his head, and then Marco's shoulder pounded into his side. The bigger United defender fell heavily against him and they both tumbled to the pitch. Cody twisted on the ground and saw that Tyler had the ball. Unfortunately, his shot was weak and right into the goalie's stomach. He caught it easily, and in one motion rolled the ball to his left outside defender parked near the sidelines.

Cody got up slowly. The collision hurt, and he thought it should've been a foul. He wasn't going to complain to the ref, though, not with the score 5–0.

Marco tapped him lightly on the back. "Great play. About time the Lions put a real striker in. Most fun I've had all game," he said.

Cody didn't know if Marco was dissing him or paying him a compliment. It probably wouldn't look good to be too chummy with Marco after his tussle with Timothy, he figured, so all he did was shrug and follow the play back to the Lions' end.

Perhaps because they knew the game was theirs, or maybe because it was fun, but United seemed determined to pass the ball amongst themselves rather than try to score. The ball ricocheted from foot to foot, and the United parents began to count the passes. Every number called out was torture to Cody. Even worse was watching his totally disorganized teammates chase the ball. Cody moved to the right side at about the forty-metre mark in the hope the ball would eventually come his way.

"Seventeen, eighteen, nineteen, twenty . . ." the United parents counted gleefully. Some began to chant "Barcelona, Barcelona, Barcelona . . ."

The United left back had the ball ten metres outside the Lions' box, with Marco backing him up. Jordan was pressuring him and Brandon had moved up to cover the winger. Over-confident and not really paying attention, the ball carrier back-heeled the ball toward Marco. But he didn't hit it hard enough, and that allowed Cody to dart in and steal it. He swept past the stationary defender.

It was a breakaway from midfield.

He dimly heard a roar from the crowd. It was a long way to dribble, so he ignored the noise and focused on making sure he at least got a shot off. Marco was fast, and he worried that he'd be caught. But by the top of the box he was still in alone. He faked a shot, and the goalie spread out his arms and leaned forward. Instinctively, Cody cut hard to the left side. The goalie stumbled as he tried to recover, and he wasn't able to close the gap. Cody took the corner no problem. The whole side of the net was open. He took great care to roll the ball into the centre of the net with his left foot.

A goal! He'd actually scored!

As if a bubble had burst, he suddenly heard everything clearly again. The Super Subs were going crazy on the sidelines. The Lions' parents clapped politely. Ian and the Dragons stood in a line, their arms folded across their chests. Cody understood they wouldn't get too excited, since it was still 5–1. Then he saw his mom hopping up and down and clapping over her head.

"Way to go, Cody! Awesome! Beautiful goal!" she hollered.

Her mission in life was to embarrass him.

Cody put his head down and jogged back to his end. Marco stood in his path. For a second, he thought Marco was going to lay into him like he did Timothy.

Instead, a smile spread across his face. "Sweet goal. You got me. Nice wheels."

He held out a fist and Cody bumped it lightly without thinking.

"Thanks. You've got an awesome team," Cody said.

"We've been together for a few years. It's a big advantage."

William, Jordan, and Brandon arrived to celebrate, and Marco walked off.

"Better late than never," William said.

"Like David said — we got one," Jordan added.

Stoked by the goal, Cody waited impatiently for the kickoff. There could be time for one more. But that was not to be. United had barely set up when the referee's whistle blasted three times. The game was over.

"Line up at centre, Lions, and shake hands, and then over to the far side to speak to Henry," Ian barked. "And hurry up."

Cody didn't understand the need to hurry, but he and his teammates hustled to centre and quickly shook hands with the United players.

"A difficult first game," Henry began, when they had gathered around him. "They're probably the strongest squad in our division, so don't get too down."

"But we're not going to win without more effort," Ian cut in. "We need more teamwork and better passes to our forwards. Timothy barely touched the ball today. Unacceptable. Midfielders are too slow to distribute, and defenders gotta be more aggressive."

"Yeah. We gotta be more aggressive," Mitch said.

"The crosses into the box were weak," Antonio's dad said.

The other Dragons chimed in: "We didn't pressure them. Gotta pressure them way more than that. Where was the ball possession? Zero ball possession. Zero."

"We also ran into some horrendous reffing," Ian said, "and that red card to Timothy was beyond anything I've ever seen."

"Ridiculous," Mitch said.

"Unbelievable."

"Stupid."

"Bizarre."

"So we gotta work harder," Ian said. "Let's think about quicker passes and better ball to our strikers — and for some of you, remember that the other team is our enemy. We don't get all friendly with them during the game."

"What team are you on, Egg-Head?" Timothy growled at Cody.

Cody didn't answer. He shouldn't have bumped Marco's fist.

"Our next practice is in two days," Henry said softly.

"Show up half an hour early," Ian said. "After that per-formance we have a lot to do."

Henry tried again. "We'll work on supporting the ball carrier and . . ."

"We gotta pass quicker to our forwards so they can run onto the ball," Ian said. "We aren't taking advantage of Timothy's pace . . . or John's."

"We definitely need faster passes," Mitch said. "Totally."

Henry sighed and folded his arms across his chest. The

Lions players interpreted that as permission to go and they wandered back to their parents. Cody had taken about ten steps when a pair of hands slowed him up.

"One goal every five minutes. Keep that up, and I see no reason you shouldn't score a couple hundred this season," Kenneth said.

"It was kinda lucky . . . with that pass . . ." Cody stammered. As if he would score that many.

"It was cool to watch — very chill. Nice deke at the end. Didn't know you could motor with the ball like that," Kenneth continued.

"Um . . . thanks."

They were about halfway across when Kenneth stopped short and gasped. "Oh my goodness. What's on your shirt?" He grabbed Luca as he went by. "Look," he said, pointing at Cody's chest. "It's terrible — a nightmare!"

Luca's hand covered his mouth and he stared in horror. Cody looked down in panic. He didn't see anything.

"What's wrong? What is it?"

"A . . . a . . . a grass stain. You've ruined it. Super Sub shirts are always perfectly clean," Kenneth said.

Cody reminded himself not to take this pair so seriously. "I'll get it washed for next game. I promise."

Kenneth tapped his heart with his right fist two times and flashed a peace sign.

"Cody, what a marvellous play." His mom had come onto the pitch. "I was so excited. Did you hear me? I was going absolutely nuts. I saw you collide with that brute of a defender. Really. You have to be more careful. Anyway, hello, boys. I'm Cody's mom, Cheryl."

Why did she do this to him? Why?

"I'm Kenneth and this is Luca. Wasn't Cody's goal awesome?"

"It was. But that United team played so well. Maybe next time."

Kenneth and Luca said their goodbyes and left. His mom continued to chatter all the way to the car, and then all the way home. It was nice that she cared so much and liked to see him do well. But couldn't she tone it down in front of his teammates? He could only imagine what Kenneth and Luca thought. He listened quietly, however, and answered the million questions she had about the goal, and the collision with Marco, and how his leg felt.

He chanced a squeeze to the back of his leg. It bothered him, but not enough to care about. A little pain was a small price to pay for his first goal since he'd gotten sick.

10

Cody jumped from the top of the staircase.

"Have you lost your mind?"

His mom was looking at him like he was a UFO.

"No big deal, Mom. I do it all the time."

She threw up her hands. "That's what I wanted to hear."

"Aw, Mom."

"Please don't do that again." She took a deep breath, and then scrunched her mouth to one side. "You've been jumping around the house all day. Why don't you do something?"

"Like what?"

"Read a book."

"I finished my book."

"So call a friend and go play."

Cody folded his arms and leaned against the wall. "I

don't have any friends here," he declared.

"What about the boys on your soccer team?"

"I barely know them — and I don't have their emails or telephone numbers."

"Please do something other than drive me crazy."

"I'll go outside . . . maybe to the park and kick the ball around."

She paused. "I . . . um . . . Why don't you . . .?" She paused again. "Okay," she said suddenly. "But no talking to strangers." She looked pale.

"I won't. No problem." He reached for his shoes. "I have a practice at six o'clock tonight. Are you driving me?"

"Yes. Your dad called and he'll be late."

"As usual."

His mom shrugged and went to her office. Cody put on his shoes, grabbed his ball from the garage, and made his way to the park. As it came into view he spotted two guys kicking a ball around. He stopped to watch. The ball arced high toward one player, a big fellow, with broad shoulders. He didn't move until the last second, reaching out deftly with his right foot and trapping the ball easily — and then he noticed the guy was wearing sandals.

Cody almost cheered.

The ball went back and his much smaller friend, a familiar-looking kid, brought the ball down with one foot also. He didn't do it quite as smoothly, but it was still a cool move. The kid kicked it back, and then the big guy one-timed it in a perfectly straight line. The kid tried his own one-timer, but it squibbed off his foot and came bounding toward the street. Cody ran across to retrieve it, dribbled it back, and kicked it with his left foot to the big fellow. Again, he brought it under control effortlessly, as if Cody had rolled it on the ground from three metres away.

The smaller player ran toward him. It was Paulo!

"You saved our ball again. Thanks, Cody," he said.

"No problem."

The two boys stared at each other.

"What're you up to?" Cody said.

"Not much. Kickin' the ball around with my papa."

So that was where Paulo got his skills.

Paulo waved his father over. "Papa, this is the boy I told you about. He got your ball back from those kids."

"Thank you for helping my Paulinho," he said, pronouncing each word carefully. "It is very nice to meet you. My name is Leandro."

He had a strong accent, way more than Paulo's.

"It was nothing," Cody replied.

Cody noticed the man's eyes drift to his skullcap, and then away. He felt himself flush deeply. Everyone was weirded out by his head.

"Do you play football?" Leandro asked in a halting tone.

"I don't play organized football, with equipment."

Paulo and his dad looked at him strangely. Then it dawned on him that they didn't mean American football. "I guess you meant soccer," Cody said. "I play a little . . . for the Lions. We play Major and we're pathetic. We've lost our first four games. Not that I play much . . . I'm a sub."

"You need my dad to coach. He played professional football in Brazil," Paulo said, with obvious pride.

"Now, Paulinho. I don't think your friend wants to hear about that."

"Papa played ten years, first for Flamengo, and then for Santos."

"I think we might have two good players right here," Leandro said. "Why don't we play together for a few minutes before I have to get back to the hospital?"

Cody thought he looked perfectly healthy. "Should we play if you're feeling sick?" Cody asked.

They both laughed.

"Thanks for your worrying. I am a doctor," Leandro said. "That is why we are here, me and my family. I am training some doctors at the hospital. We are here for six months. Do you know St. Mary's?"

Did he ever! That's where he'd had his cancer treatments. Cody simply nodded.

"I studied in America," he continued, "which is why Paulinho can speak English so well." He rubbed his chin and grinned. "I wish I could speak like him. We live in Brazil, and I do not often get a chance to practise."

"You speak very well," Cody objected. "Besides, you speak two languages, English and Spanish."

They laughed again. Cody wondered what he'd said that was so funny.

Paulo passed him the ball. "We speak Portuguese in Brazil, not Spanish."

His dad snatched the ball away. "Gentlemen, this is the time for some keep away."

He dribbled to his right, Paulo hot on his heels. At first, Cody was tentative. It felt strange to play soccer with someone else's dad; Cody didn't really play sports with his own dad. But it didn't take long for him to get into it, mostly because no matter how hard they tried the two boys could not get the ball. It seemed glued to his foot, sandals and all. Finally, Paulo wrapped his arms around his dad's legs, and Cody swooped in and took the ball. Leandro laughed and patted Paulo's back.

"That was fun. But now we must go. I need to shower and get back to work."

"Come on, Papa. We just got here."

"We've been playing for half an hour. That's short for a child, but a long time for my old bones." Leandro reached into his pocket and pulled out his wallet. "Here's a card with our email address and phone number," he said, handing it to Cody. "We should arrange for you and Paulo to play football together again. It's tough on Paulo because he does not know other children here. It was nice meeting you, and thanks again for retrieving my ball. Paulinho, say goodbye to Cody."

"Give us two more minutes to kick the ball around," Paulo pleaded. With a mischievous grin, he added, "You can rest your old bones on the soft grass while we play."

Leandro threw his head back and laughed deeply. "You win. Five more minutes." He winked at Cody. "When I was young, I, too, sometimes asked my papa to play five minutes more." In a mock-serious tone, he ordered, "Now, let me see some one-touch."

Paulo dropped the ball onto his right foot and bounced it several times. Then he began bouncing it off the outside of his foot. The ball flew higher and higher, and after ten hits he kneed it over to Cody. He controlled it off his chest, and tried to bounce it off his right foot like Paulo. He did it twice, and then it caromed off his toe and rolled to the side. Red-faced, he scampered over to retrieve it.

"My Paulo has got a lot of tricks," Leandro called out. "I see your strength is running. Use your legs, Cody. The tricks will come later."

That made him feel better and he punched the ball to Paulo, who one-timed it back. In no time they were zooming about, touching the ball only once without letting it come to a stop. Cody was having a great time, and all three of them laughed when he had to make a few crazed runs to corral a wild pass before it stopped rolling. The only thing that worried him was a twinge in the back of his right leg after he used it once for a long pass. He hardly ever kicked hard with his right leg and still it hurt. When would it get back to normal?

After what seemed a lot longer than five minutes to Cody, Leandro got up and pointed to the street. He nodded approvingly. "If I wait for you to stop playing I will be here all day. You're a good player, Cody. Very fast. Hard on the ball. Good control. You would make a good team with Paulo. He has good ball skills and you have the foot speed."

"Thanks, Leandro," Cody said.

"Don't forget to send me an email, and we can do this again," Paulo's dad said. "Come on, Paulinho. We must go."

"Not my fault, Papa. I told you we should go ten minutes ago."

Leandro laughed and wrapped his arm around Paulo's shoulders.

"See ya, Cody," Paulo called out as they left.

Cody waved back. Leandro never took his arm off Paulo's shoulders. Cody felt uncomfortable, and turned away. How amazing would it be to have a dad who'd been a professional soccer player?

He wandered to a bench and watched three boys taking shots on the basketball court. He didn't really feel like going home. They might let him play if he asked, and then they could play two-on-two. But they were probably old friends; he didn't know them; they'd wonder about his skullcap . . . Now that he thought about it he didn't really feel like playing basketball.

After awhile he slipped his hand into his pocket and pulled out the card. Should he actually send the email? Kinda strange — like organizing a play date between little kids. On the other hand, he'd always be up for playing soccer with those two.

He looked at the card again.

11

"I told you the practice was at seven."

"I realize that, Cheryl. But I got held up on a conference call."

"From the President of the United States?"

"Amusing."

"Not in the least. Get engaged with family life, please. You promised to be here for dinner, and then drive him to practice."

"Like I said, I wanted to. I have a job. Things happen."

"They always do with you."

"Whatever. I'm here now and I'll take him."

"You haven't had dinner."

"I'm not hungry."

Cody listened from the top of the stairs. His stomach felt sick, not like a tummy ache but deeper, a tingling, spidery sensation. As if his parents arguing all the time about driving him to practice wasn't bad enough, the soccer itself wasn't much fun. The Lions kept losing, game after game, and Ian and Mitch and the other Dragons kept getting angrier and angrier. After the last game, a 4–1 loss, he'd seen Ian and Henry yelling at each other in the parking lot. He couldn't hear what they were saying, but from the expressions on their faces he could tell neither was very happy.

"Cody. C'mon. We're going to be late," his dad barked.

"Okay. Be down in a second."

Cody went to the washroom and splashed cold water on his face. He rubbed his eyes, peering at his face closely in the mirror. When he was satisfied his dad wouldn't see how upset he'd been from hearing them argue, he wiped his face dry, grabbed his gear from his bedroom, and headed downstairs.

★★★

Jordan teed the ball up for a corner. A group of players jockeyed for position in front of the goal. Cody slipped in behind Antonio. He'd almost headed in the last one, before David punched it away at the last second.

"Hurry up," Timothy bellowed. "Practice is gonna start soon."

Jordan struck the ball, and it sailed high and wide. John leapt but was nowhere near it. Cody drifted back a few steps and readied himself. This one was perfect, and too far out for David to interfere.

Antonio's elbow smashed into his ribs, taking his breath away. The ball thudded to the ground behind him.

"Get outta my way, Egg-Head," Antonio said.

"You'll break your shell, anyway," said Timothy.

"Remember what happened to Humpty Dumpty," Tyler added.

Cody struggled to control himself. The dissing was getting bad, especially when Kenneth and Luca weren't around, like now.

"You talk too much, Humpty. Keep quiet for once," said Timothy, and he nudged John.

Cody knew he was turning red. He always did when he got nervous. He tried desperately to think of a comeback — and not to cry.

"Yeah, shut up, already," John said, and he and Timothy laughed.

"You guys should do the shutting up," David said. His hands were on his hips, his eyes blazing. "I think he's the only guy on this team who can actually score."

Cody wasn't sure if David was defending him, or just mad that the Lions had lost their first six games. After Cody's goal against United, only Timothy, on a penalty shot and a set piece, had scored again.

"Don't give up five goals a game and maybe we'll win," Timothy said.

David snorted. "We maybe get two shots all game, and the other teams are getting twenty. The ball never leaves our end, and when a miracle happens and we get possession, we lose it right away. I say Cody should be a striker."

Cody's chest felt heavy.

"You wanna put Humpty up front?" Timothy said, as if it were the most ridiculous thing he'd ever heard. "This ain't the circus."

"His name's Cody," David said. "And those aren't the only changes I'd make."

"Who cares?" Antonio said.

Jordan launched another kick into the box, but no one moved and it bounced off to the sidelines. "What's the deal?" he called out. "Are we still playing?"

"I still say Humpty talks too much," John said, and he started to giggle, and soon Timothy, Antonio, Tyler, and a few others joined in.

Cody was going to cry; he knew it. He turned away and walked to where Kenneth and Luca were passing the ball at midfield. He quickly wiped his eyes — a couple of tears had managed to leak out.

He heard the sound of cleats pounding behind him. Would they ever leave him alone?

"Cody, wait up."

David looked mad. "Forget them. They're total losers."

Cody wondered why David was being so nice. He was the best athlete on the team and really popular, and his incredible saves were the only reason the Lions didn't lose ten-nothing every game.

"I . . . um . . . I don't care. I know they're idiots. It's just . . ." He prayed he wouldn't cry in front of David. "I didn't do anything to them . . ."

"It's cause you're the best striker we've got and Timothy and John know it. Especially John. He's useless."

"Thanks. I don't know. Maybe."

Cody felt self-conscious. "The best striker on the team" — did he really think that?

Kenneth and Luca came over to join them. "I was thinking the Super Subs should take up knitting, since we have time on our hands," Kenneth was saying. "We could knit everyone matching sweaters, so we can stay warm when it gets nippy at night. Think we should make it hoodies?"

Kenneth held out his hands as if he really wanted their opinion. David and Luca began laughing, and when Kenneth did, too Cody realized he'd almost taken Kenneth seriously again. Lucky he hadn't said anything.

Kenneth noticed he wasn't laughing, though, and he said, "You're a tough audience, Cody. Don't worry. I can do better."

"It's those losers," David said, thumbing back to the goal. "They're going on about the Humpty thing, and it's getting so bogus."

Luca looked downfield. "Who was it?"

"It doesn't matter," Cody said weakly.

It didn't seem like they heard him, however.

"I'm gonna talk to the coach," Kenneth said.

"Like he'll listen," David replied. "He does whatever Ian says."

"I'm sure John's dad will help," Kenneth said, and they laughed, except for Cody, again. He just wanted them to change the subject.

"Did John even touch the ball last game?" David fumed. "I mean, they told my parents how great this team was last year, and how we were gonna win the provincials and tournaments, and we had this scoring machine named Timothy . . . and the best players are on the bench!"

"Hey, don't break up the Super Subs," Kenneth said. "It's the only time we have for knitting, and I'm about to start a book club."

The whistle was blown and Henry waved for everyone to come to the sidelines. Cody trudged behind his teammates, a little less miserable than before. At least three guys on the team didn't think he was some kind of freak.

Timothy was singing a song. *I am the Walrus . . . I am the Walrus . . . I am the Eggman . . . Do do de do . . .*

It was an old Beatles song.

And David was right. Henry wouldn't do a thing.

"I want to show you something," Henry began, as he held up the whiteboard. "We need to get more pressure on their goalie, so I want to go with a 4-3-3, with Cody up front as the third forward."

Cody   Timothy   John

Tyler   Brandon   Jordan

Nathan   William   Antonio   Michael

David

Cody saw Timothy turn his eyes up to the sky. "Dad, come on. That's dumb. We scored a lot last year, and we could this year if we just played better."

"I know, Timmer," Ian said. "Let's stick with the usual formation, Henry. We need better support and more passes to Timothy and John. I've told you that a thousand times."

"Don't need Humpty on forward," John muttered.

"Let's focus on winning," Antonio's dad said.

"We give up too much ball in our end," another Dragon said. "And our crosses still suck."

Henry's shoulder's sagged. He looked so tired and sad that Cody almost felt worse for his coach than for himself.

"We need a forward who can actually score," David said loudly.

"Stop the ball for once," Timothy said.

"Score!" David shot back.

"Quiet down, boys," Ian said loudly. "We're gonna stick with the 4-4-2, and in this practice I want to work on the long ball up the side to John, or work it into the middle for Timothy's big shot. We must've scored ten goals last year with that play."

Henry was shaking his head the entire time Ian spoke. "Last year Timothy and John were bigger than everyone," Henry said. "The other boys are catching up. The long ball is not working. We need to control it, build up the attack . . ."

"We've got more talent on this team than anyone," Ian said. "It's just a crazy slump and it'll end if you do what I tell you. All we need is the right coaching and more effort."

Henry looked off in the distance. He tucked his

whiteboard under his arm and turned to face the players. "I've been coaching for over forty years. I do it because I love the game and enjoy getting to know the players and the parents, and it's been my pleasure to coach until now. But I haven't been doing a good job. I can't get you to play how I want. The teamwork isn't there. The passing isn't there. We aren't playing together as a unit. But what bothers me more than anything is that I don't like how some boys are treating their fellow teammates, and I can't seem to stop it. A team can't win unless it sticks together, and that means on and off the pitch. If there's one thing I hope you'll remember, it's that.

"All this is to say I have to quit as your coach. Good luck, boys, and I'm sorry I let you down."

He walked away without another word.

Cody felt helpless. What now? Would Ian coach? What a nightmare.

Ian stepped forward. "This was going to happen sooner than later, I'm sorry to say. I just didn't want it to happen like this. He's a nice fellow, don't get me wrong, and we didn't want to hurt his feelings. But me and the Dragons have come to realize that he might be a bit old to coach at this level. To play Major we need a high-performance coach."

"Amen."

"You said it."

"About time."

The Dragons were all nodding, the expressions on their faces full of drama.

Ian winked at the players. "I'll let you in on a huge

secret. I was gonna wait until I had a chance to speak to Henry in private, but after his little hissy fit, well, I guess this is the best time. We've been talking to a new coach for a while, me and the Dragons — a former professional player. He's agreed to come on board. At first, he was going to be the assistant, even though I was going to get him to be the real coach behind the scenes. Now he can take over. I'll run the practice today, and on Thursday your new coach will be here." He clapped his hands a bunch of times. "Awesome. Now let's start with some fitness."

Timothy, Antonio, and John booed.

"I know some of you are fit, but . . ." Ian made a sour face, "some guys could use a bit of training. So everyone on the goal line and we'll do a run down the field."

Cody felt like he was carrying a fifty-pound weight on his back, he was so tired all of a sudden.

"At least that solves the problem of whether we should talk to Henry or not," Kenneth joked as they walked to the goal line.

"I guess," Cody said.

Kenneth did a few windmills with his arms. "With Ian in charge maybe we'll have time to do a few crafts." He stuck a finger up in the air and opened his eyes wide. "I've got it — we can get into scrapbooking."

Cody laughed to be polite.

Kenneth pursed his lips and rolled his neck. "Don't let Timothy and that bunch bug ya. They're idiots — we know that."

Cody felt the tears coming back and fought to control them. It all seemed so unfair and hopeless. "I don't care about them. But I don't know about this team and . . . maybe I'll just forget about it . . ."

"Don't give up," Kenneth said in an urgent tone. "We're getting a new coach. At least wait until he's here. It might get better. I mean, it can't get worse."

Cody looked at Kenneth in surprise. He'd never heard him so serious. "How will it get better with Ian's friend coaching?"

Kenneth surprised him again. The kid who never stopped talking didn't answer. He scowled and kicked at the ground with his cleats.

"On your marks . . . get set . . ."

A bunch of guys, led by Timothy, took off. Ian didn't even bother with the "Go." Cody followed along at a jog. He wasn't about to kill himself for Ian. He looked over to see if Henry had left. He was still on the sidelines talking to some parents.

Kenneth came up beside him. "You can't leave the Super Subs," he said. "Not before we start our scrapbooks. Promise me that. At least one more practice."

Cody smiled weakly. "Okay. I don't want to mess with your crafts."

What difference would one practice make?

12

Cody's finger lingered over the return key. He'd rewritten the email ten times, but it still sounded dorky.

Paulo,

Hi,

I'm usually around most days. Maybe we can play football again at the park sometime. Email me back if you can.

Cody

"I said off the computer ten minutes ago. Come on. Don't make me nag." His mom stood in the doorway.

He tapped the return key. The email was gone, and he couldn't take it back. "Sorry, Mom. Lost track of time."

She came into the den. "I'm sure that's the reason. Anyway, don't forget we're going to dinner later at Grandma's and Grandpa's. You might want to shower up, and wear your nice grey pants and that new blue shirt I got you."

"Mom, it's just Grandma and Grandpa."

"You can still look nice."

An email popped up — from Paulo! He clicked on it.

"Cody, I said turn it off!"

"I will," he said. "Just a sec. It's an email from that kid I met in the park. He wants to know if I can play soccer . . . in the park . . . now."

Her head tilted to one side, "Who is this Paulo, exactly?"

"He's from Brazil and I met him at the park. He plays soccer, and we kicked the ball around. Like I told you."

"Anything else?"

"Not really, other than his dad was a professional soccer player."

She ran a hand through her hair, which usually meant she was thinking.

"I need to go shopping to pick up a few things," she said. "I can give you lift."

"That's okay. I can walk."

"Don't be silly. It's no problem."

"But . . . I can walk easily."

"Let's go, Cody. I'll come around to get you in about half an hour. You have to shower before dinner and I don't want to be late. Your Aunt Beth and Uncle Michael are coming, too."

He groaned. "Does that mean the Tasmanian Devil will be there?"

"Your cousin's name is Adam — and he's not so bad. You'll have fun together."

"I think I feel sick and I can't go to dinner."

She grinned. "What about Paulo?"

She had him. "Okay," he said. "But do you have to drive me?"

"Yes," she said firmly.

★★★

The car rolled to a stop. His mom took off her seat belt.

"I thought you were going shopping," he said.

She opened her door. "I'll just come and say hi to Paulo. I'd like to meet your friend."

That was her plan all along, he realized. Paulo was going to think he was totally lame. He lagged behind as they walked to the park. "He's not here yet," he said, hoping she might leave.

"We're early. Come on. Let's kick the ball around."

"Mom!"

She slapped the ball out of his hands and began dribbling.

"You try to stop me," she said, heading toward him.

"Mom!"

"You've got no chance, by the way."

He made a token effort to stop her, and she slid the ball between his legs and ran around to get it. He turned, and before he was ready she'd spun, slipped the ball between his legs again, and was running in the opposite direction — laughing.

She turned to face him, one foot on the ball. "Not bad for an old lady, huh?"

If Paulo had seen that he'd never want to play with him again.

"I'll give you one more chance," she said.

He got mad. Why didn't she listen to him? Why couldn't he come to the park by himself? Cody swung his left foot wildly at the ball and hit his mom's shin.

"Cody!"

She knelt on one knee, and rubbed her leg. "Cody. That really hurt." She had tears in her eyes, and he could tell she was in pain. What a disaster. Never should have sent that email.

"Yo, Cody. Sorry we're late."

Paulo and his father waved and were walking over. Paulo kicked his ball to Cody.

"Mom, can you get up?" he whispered. He didn't want them to know what had happened. He was feeling crummy about it, too. She gave him a dirty look as she stood up.

"Hi. I'm Cody's mom, Cheryl. You must be Paulo."

"I am. Nice to meet you. This is my papa, Leandro."

"Nice to meet you, Leandro."

"It's a pleasure, Cheryl," Leandro said. "Your son is a very good player — very fast."

"Thanks — and I know," she said.

The two adults laughed.

"I have a few errands to run, but then I have to steal Cody away. We have dinner plans at his grandparents'," she said.

"We have to go also," Leandro said. "My sister is leaving for São Paulo. We have to take her to the airport."

"Is that where you're from?" she asked.

"No. We're from a town in the north — Belém," Leandro said.

"Have you moved here?" she said.

Cody and Paulo drifted off, passing the ball back and forth with short kicks.

"How are the Lions doing?" Paulo said.

"Same as usual — awful. We've lost six in a row."

Paulo laughed. "Does the coach let you play yet?"

Cody laughed also, and felt himself relax a little. "Not yet. I'm still waiting for my big break. There are a few of us subs who never play. We call ourselves the Super Subs." Cody stopped short. That sounded dumb. Paulo wouldn't care.

"Let's do some one-timers and see how many we can do without messing up," Paulo said. They did that until Paulo called out, "How about we see how many times we can pass the ball to each other in the air?" He began bouncing the ball from foot to foot, and then over to Cody. Cody bounced it on his left foot a couple of times, and then, not wanting to be the first to blow it, gave it back. Paulo kept joking around and laughing when the ball fell to the ground. He wasn't taking it seriously, and soon Cody didn't either. They began to keep count, and after a few tries had made it to seventeen touches.

"Hey, Papa. Head's up," Paulo shouted. He sent a high kick toward his father.

Leandro controlled it easily and bounced it a few times on each foot. He tapped it over to Cody's mom.

She began to bounce the ball on her right foot. Cody could barely watch, convinced she was going to embarrass him again.

"I am very impressed," Leandro said. "I can see where Cody received his football skills."

"I was always playing one sport or another when I was a kid," she said, still bouncing the ball on her right foot, "but soccer was always my favourite." She kicked it to Cody in a perfect arc. All he had to do was stick out his foot to stop it.

She sure can play, Cody thought.

"I think it is time for us to be going, Paulinho," Leandro said.

Paulo slapped his thigh with his hand. "You said we could play until four o'clock."

Leandro tapped his watch. "I don't want Aunt Maria to think we forgot about her."

"My goodness," Cody's mom said. "I completely lost track of time. We have to run. I need to get some flowers for dinner, and . . . I guess I'll have to do my shopping another day."

"Your mom has been telling me about your football team," Leandro said to Cody. "She knows a lot about the game, and I agree with her that your new coach should give you a chance to play at the striker position. You have the . . . How do you say — the wheels?"

"You got it, Papa,' Paulo said.

"Maybe you can ask your coach if Paulo can play, even if only for practising," Leandro said. "I want Paulo to meet some other boys, and I know he's not happy missing football."

"That's a wonderful idea," his mom enthused. "There's a practice in two days. We can ask the manager. I'm sure it won't be a problem. It would be nice to have Paulo on the team. Would you like to play?" she asked him.

Paulo flashed a toothy grin. "That would be great. I'd love to play with Cody. We can both be Super Subs."

Cody could've killed her. Of course he'd love to have Paulo on the team. But when your nicknames are Egg-Head and Chicken-Leg you don't exactly ask the manager for something like that. He could only imagine what Ian would say — or, way worse, Timothy. Now he was totally on the spot. How could he get out of this one?

His mom held up her cell phone. "Leandro and I have each other's numbers, and you've already exchanged emails, so we can do this again — and hopefully you'll both be Lions soon."

"That would be terrific," Leandro said.

They said their goodbyes, and Cody and his mom headed for the car. As they got to the curb, Paulo called out, "Let me know what your manager says."

Cody nodded and waved back. On the way to the flower shop his mom kept talking about Paulo's family. After his soccer career, Leandro had gone to school and become a doctor. Paulo's mom was a journalist, and had travelled the world working for a Brazilian television station. They were here for six months while Leandro taught at the hospital.

"He knows Dr. Charya very well," she said. "She's a leader in her field, which makes me feel even better. She was terrific with us, and Leandro says she's absolutely brilliant."

"You spoke about me, then," he said. "About . . . the hospital."

"Of course. He's a doctor."

"But it's none of his business. He'll tell Paulo and . . . it's none of his business. You can't go around telling people everything, Mom. I can't believe you sometimes."

"I think you're overreacting, honey. He's a doctor, a professional, and he won't speak about your medical condition." She reached out and squeezed his shoulder. "But I apologize all the same. I shouldn't have talked about it without your permission."

"Okay . . . and sorry I got so mad."

"That's okay, dear. We're all entitled to lose our tempers once in a while and . . . Look! A parking spot!" She swerved to the right and parked. "Do you want to come in?"

"I'll wait in the car," he said.

He stared out the window. Things had gotten messed in a hurry. Henry was gone; Paulo expected him to ask Ian for a tryout; Ian would laugh him off the pitch; Timothy would invent a few new nicknames; and he wasn't too sure about Leandro keeping his cancer a secret from Paulo.

Why'd he promise Kenneth to come out to the next practice? He needed a way out of this. After some thinking he came up with a plan. First off, he'd tell Ian that Paulo was a striker. Ian would say no, obviously, and that would be the end of it. Then he'd pretend to hurt his leg; his mom wanted him to stop playing, anyway. He'd quit, and it would be over.

His mom came back in and they drove home. His plan made him feel better for a while, but an uneasy feeling soon returned. He spent the rest of the drive trying to figure out why.

13

Cody hopped up and down to loosen up. For what seemed the millionth time, he reviewed the plan he'd come up with in the car. At one end Jordan was kicking corners. He didn't dare go over, not after last practice, but standing off to the side made him feel kinda dumb. He pulled a water bottle from the holder and pretended to take a big sip. There were a few balls lying around, and he began bouncing one up in the air.

"You must be on the Lions," a man said to him from behind.

That was a strange. Even though he was a sub, a parent should know who was on the team.

"What position?" the man asked.

Cody snuck a quick glance. He'd never seen him before. The man was on the short side, but he looked strong and really fit.

"I'm a forward," Cody said.

"Are you Timothy?"

Cody flushed. "No. I'm Cody Dorsett. I'm a sub. Timothy is the guy over there — number ten — with the red hair."

"Dorsett? I was looking over the stats. Didn't you score a goal?"

"Um . . . Yeah . . . in the first game. It was lucky, though. A defender passed it right to me."

He waved him off. "We've only got three goals all season. You're practically our leading scorer." He held out his hand. Cody felt funny, but he shook it. "My name's Trevor. Nice to meet you, Cody."

It suddenly dawned on him that he was their new coach.

"Could you do me a favour and tell the lads to come over? I want to go over a few things before practice."

Cody was immediately filled with dread. They'd just love the chance to dis him. The new coach looked at him strangely, and then gestured for him to come closer.

"Don't worry about it," he said. "I have a better idea." He reached into his pocket and blew his whistle. Jordan kicked one more, and John and Antonio went up for it. John had position, but the ball skidded off the top of his head and bounced to the far sideline.

Trevor grunted and crossed his arms. "See what he did wrong?"

Cody shook his head.

"He let the ball come to him rather than attacking it. You need to go after the ball in the air to control it." He paused for a moment. "Was that John, by any chance?"

"Yeah."

He grunted again. "Interesting."

Soon the rest of the Lions arrived.

"Have a knee, lads. Come along. No dawdling."

Kenneth knelt beside Cody. "Why didn't you come practise corners?" he asked.

As if it weren't obvious! He didn't say that, though. "I was talking to the new coach," he said.

Kenneth's eyes grew wide. "I think that's Trevor Ferguson."

"I know his name's Trevor," Cody offered.

"Then it's him. He played pro for maybe ten years in Europe and in the MSL."

"Let me introduce myself. My name is Trevor Ferguson."

Kenneth elbowed Cody in the ribs.

"I've been given the opportunity to coach you for the rest of the season."

Ian and Mitch came running over, both out of breath, with the other Dragons close behind.

"Hey, Trevor. Let me introduce you to the team," Ian said.

"That's been taken care of," Trevor said.

Ian's head jerked back "Okay. Sure. Right. Fabulous. Boys, I'm totally excited about our new coach. He played . . ."

"Ian. No need to talk about ancient history. I'd rather focus on soccer. First, I want to run through my philosophy for attacking and defending. Then we'll scrimmage to give me a chance to check out the skill and fitness level."

"Both are very high, I can tell you that," Ian said.

"Very, very skilled," Mitch added.

Trevor stepped forward. "That's great. We'll also see the commitment level."

"You'll find commitment is not lacking on this squad," Ian said. "Timothy's a bull on the ball and . . ."

"Super," Trevor said. "Thanks. We'll do some fitness, and then before we scrimmage I'll review the 4–3–3 formation, which . . ."

Ian cleared his throat. "Sorry to interrupt, Trevor, but if you remember, we play a 4–4–2. With Timothy and John up front, we have enough firepower and it . . ." His voice faded away. Trevor was looking at him rather intently and he didn't appear too impressed.

"We led the league in scoring last season," Mitch offered.

"We're not leading this season," Trevor replied. "Now, gentlemen, how about you let me handle the coaching, and you take care of the managing." He flashed the two managers a thumbs-up. "Can I have that team list, please?"

Ian handed him a sheet of paper.

Trevor looked at the list. "I thought you were allowed eighteen players. I only see seventeen names."

"That's right," Ian said, his hands waving in the air. "We kept one spot open because I had my eye on a couple of players who might want to sign with us. It was only prudent."

"But you haven't filled the spot?" Trevor said directly.

"Not yet."

"But isn't there a deadline?"

"It's in about ten days," Ian squirmed. "We're still

looking. I have a few possibilities; we can talk after practice."

"With our fitness level, it's not a problem, anyway," Mitch said.

"He's right," Ian said. "Not even an issue. Our starters can run forever. We've been . . ."

"I'll see about that fitness," Trevor said. He looked at the players. "I promise you one thing. We'll be the fittest team in the league whether we win a game or not. But of course, you guys are fit already . . ." His voice trailed off. "You only have two forwards listed."

"Timothy and John are our strikers," Ian stated.

"And only one goalie?"

"David's the best in the league. The other guys at the tryouts weren't up to our standards," Ian said.

Trevor lowered the paper slowly. "You and Mitch can help by being linesmen when we scrimmage. Follow me, lads," he called out, setting off at a fast pace.

★★★

Trevor wasn't kidding about the fitness. Cody rubbed his side where a cramp had been torturing him while he did wind sprints up and down the pitch. The guy was relentless, constantly asking them to run faster. Cody had never worked so hard in his life.

"The man's insane," Kenneth wheezed. "I think he escaped from a mental institution and spends his time trying to kill young soccer players."

Luca tried to say something, but he was breathing too

hard. He barely managed a nod.

"It's your fault," Cody said to Kenneth. "I should've quit after last practice."

Kenneth shook his head. "You can't quit. It's against the Super Subs' rules."

The whistle sounded. "Can I have Cody, Kenneth, Anthony, Luca, Ryan, and Jacob over here? You're Team B. I need two volunteers from the starters to play on their side," Trevor announced.

William and Jordan put up their hands.

"I'll play with them, too," David said.

"You're the goalie, right?" Trevor asked.

David nodded.

"Stick with the others for now," Trevor said. He gathered the starters around him. "You boys are Team A. I understand you've played every game this season, and I want to see you together. Keep in mind that all the positions are up for grabs, and I don't have too much time to make decisions. This weekend we have a tournament. I'll assess skills over the next two practices and the best man wins, so go for it."

Kenneth pulled Cody and Luca aside. "This is our chance. It's time for the Super Subs to retire."

Cody had never seen Kenneth look so intense. "I don't think Ian will let us play," he said.

"Forget him," Kenneth said. "Do you think Trevor sounds like a guy who listens to Ian?"

Cody definitely did not.

"Hey, Anthony, come here," Kenneth said. "Are you stoked, or what? We gotta bring it."

"Hopefully this coach isn't as moronic as Henry," Anthony said.

Kenneth took no notice of Anthony's mood, as usual. "My only worry is I might have to cancel the book club."

Luca let out a gasp. "Anything but that," he said.

Trevor was heading to midfield. "Line it up, lads. We've wasted enough time talking already," he shouted.

Cody wondered exactly when they'd wasted any time. William, Luca, and Jacob hung back. Kenneth, Anthony, and Ryan were at midfield. Cody figured that meant he was supposed to be the forward. He hovered around centre and waited.

"Team A has to hit the post to score," Trevor said. "Now let's play some soccer!" He threw the ball overhand to William. Timothy charged after him, John flanked to the right. William showed some patience, allowing Timothy to get close before drilling the ball wide right to Luca, who one-timed it square to Kenneth.

"Cody, yours."

Cody tore into an open seam and took Kenneth's pass, spinning around and charging up field. He spotted Jordan near midfield and sent the ball over. Jordan trapped it with his right foot and lofted a left-footer to Ryan.

Kenneth and Jordan continued to move forward in support, with William and Luca hanging back. Timothy and John hovered near centre, which was no surprise to Cody. But that meant the middle would be wide open, and Cody decided to exploit that. He put it into high gear. Ryan anticipated the play and snapped a sharp cross toward him.

The cross was a bit long and Cody had to stretch for it.

It tipped the top of his right foot, and he felt a twinge in the back of his right leg. He knew he should shoot, but the twinge made him hesitate and he dribbled another step so he could shot with his left. That gave Antonio time to knock the ball away.

"A little quicker, Cody," Trevor shouted.

Head down, Cody jogged back.

"Pick up the pace, boys. Soccer is a fitness sport!" Trevor continued, and he kept at them to run, run, run. Team B took it to heart, and despite being outnumbered, they more than held their own, even dominating at times, maintaining possession for long stretches. Cody had several solid runs and he forced David to make two spectacular saves, one of which hit his extended right arm and bounced off the goal post. Just when Cody thought he couldn't run any more, he heard Trevor say the words he longed to hear: "Bring it in, lads."

Practice was over.

Cody slunk to the ground fighting for breath, sweat dripping down his forehead and stinging his eyes. Kenneth and Luca flopped next to him.

"Great practice," Ian said loudly. He sounded a little nervous to Cody. The Dragons huddled behind him. "We have another practice Wednesday, and then . . ."

Trevor laughed and slung his arm across Ian's shoulder. Ian winced.

"I'm having trouble keeping you fellas off the pitch, ain't I? Maybe one of you can be the eighteenth player?"

Ian laughed awkwardly.

"I just . . . with the tournament this weekend . . . I need

to go over . . ." Ian looked at Mitch.

"Yes. We . . . what with the tournament . . . we need to . . ." Mitch seemed to run out of words.

"I always like to debrief my team after practice," Trevor said. "Why don't you and Mitch set up on the sidelines, and I'll send the lads over when I'm done."

". . . Yeah. . . . Sure thing . . . That could work. I just . . ." Ian's shoulders slumped.

"Fabulous," Trevor said. "I only need two minutes." He turned to the players. "I didn't expect you to be able to play full-out yet. I can tell you're not in shape for that. But I did want to see which of you were willing to try. Some of you did — and some didn't.

"We have one more practise after which I'll pick the tournament starting lineup. As I said before, no one's guaranteed a spot and no one's out of the running, either." He nodded emphatically. "You'll earn a starting position by working even harder at Wednesday's practice, so consider yourselves warned." He thumbed over his shoulder. "I believe your managers want to talk to you," he said, the corners of his mouth rising ever so slightly.

Kenneth and Luca began walking to the sidelines. Cody struggled a bit to get up. His leg was stiff and he was trashed from the practice. Trevor offered his hand and pulled him to his feet. Cody was impressed by the strength in his arm.

"Thanks, Coach," he mumbled.

"Not a problem. You keep up that effort level and I think you'll get a chance to add to your goal total this weekend," Trevor said.

Cody kept his eyes down, even though he was totally stoked by Trevor's compliment.

"Wish we had more depth at forward," Trevor continued. "I'd like to have more than three."

Paulo!

He could play forward.

Cody took a deep breath and blurted out, "I know this kid named Paulo who's looking for a team. He's amazing, and his dad played professional soccer in Brazil. They call it football there."

There he went again saying something lame when he was nervous. Trevor obviously knew what they called soccer in Brazil; and how had he forgotten about his plan? What if Paulo told Timothy about his cancer? What would his nickname be then?

"Have you played . . . *football* with this Paulo?" Trevor said.

"A little bit, sure, at the park, with his dad. He's really good . . . Paulo, I mean. His dad is, too. He's really good with the ball — Paulo, I mean."

Trevor ran his hand across his chin. "And you say he doesn't have a team?"

Cody shook his head. "He's here with his family from Brazil. I think he'd like to play, even if he could only practise."

Trevor didn't answer right away. Finally, he said, "How about you tell your friend Paulo to come to our Wednesday practice. If he's half as good as you say, we could use him. Can you do that?"

"No problem, Coach. He'll come. I'll call him tonight."

"Very cool," Trevor said. "I'll see you both on Wednesday, then."

Cody nodded and headed to the sidelines where his teammates and the parents had gathered to hear Ian's announcements about the tournament. Kenneth handed him a sheet of paper with the times and locations of the games. Cody took a deep breath. Maybe this was better than his plan. Trevor seemed like a straight-up coach; and it would be awesome if Paulo made the team.

He could only pray Paulo kept quiet about the cancer stuff.

Cody and Paulo waited at the edge of the parking lot for Trevor.

"Cody. Who's your friend?"

Kenneth and Luca came over, passing a ball to each other. When they were five metres away Luca punched it hard to Paulo. He stopped it coolly with his right foot. Cody could tell Kenneth and Luca were impressed.

"This is Paulo," Cody said. "He's gonna try out."

"Awesome. Did you guys play on the same team last season?" Kenneth asked.

"Nah," Paulo said. "Cody and me, we play together at the park, and he said there was a spot."

"We could use the help," Luca said. "What position do you play?"

Before Paulo could answer, a voice called out. "What're

you guys doing? Let's warm up." Anthony glared at them, his hands on his hips.

"Come say hi to Paulo," Kenneth said. "He's Cody's bud and is gonna try out."

Anthony's face hardened. "Tryouts are over. Why's he here?"

Kenneth and Luca looked to Cody.

"We didn't sign eighteen players," Cody said. "I told Trevor about Paulo. He's really good." Anthony seemed unimpressed. "His dad played professional soccer in Brazil," Cody added.

Anthony gave Cody a quick look. "Okay. Whatever. Are we gonna kick the ball around or what?"

No one answered.

"Give me the ball, then," Anthony demanded.

Paulo rolled it to him. Anthony backheeled it and spun around, dribbling toward the far end where guys were drilling shots at David.

A pickup truck rolled into the parking lot. "Coach is here," Cody said. He felt his nervousness level rise about ten notches. "I guess we should . . . or me and Paulo should . . . we should go over to . . . over there."

Paulo flashed a toothy grin and headed toward the parked truck. Cody followed, as did Kenneth and Luca. Trevor hopped out and grabbed a large string bag full of balls from the cab.

"Perfect timing," he said to them. "I need a volunteer for these." Cody took the bag and slung it over his shoulder. "Are you going to introduce me to your friend?" Trevor asked.

"This is Paulo," Cody began, "the guy I was telling you about."

"What position do you play?" Trevor asked.

Paulo laughed. "It would be fun to just be able to practise with the team. I know you're into the season already. I'll play wherever you need me."

Trevor held up his hand. "That's a good answer. But I presume you have a preference."

"Forward, I guess."

"Cody, toss me a ball," Trevor said.

Cody dug a ball out of the string bag.

"Show me what you got, kid," Trevor said. He tossed a ball in the air.

Cody wished he could be as cool as Paulo just once in his life. The ball wizard bounced it off each foot a few times, then off each knee, and finally he punted it four metres straight up — and caught it in the crook of his right foot and shin, as if it were the easiest thing in the world. Paulo slowly lowered the ball to the ground and casually flicked it to Cody.

Kenneth let out a low whistle.

"You just earned yourself a tryout," Trevor said.

A huge smile crossed Paulo's face.

"Let's get to practice, lads," Trevor said, and he set off to the pitch.

Cody struggled to think of something to say to Paulo as they followed behind. Fortunately, Kenneth had no problem breaking the ice.

"I'd give that a ten out of ten on the awesome factor scale," Kenneth said to Paulo. "You've got what this team needs — talent. We get you and Cody up front, we might actually score — maybe even a goal!"

"Who are the strikers?" Paulo asked in a serious tone.

Luca snorted. "We got the dynamic duo, Timothy and John, and I think they've scored two goals all year."

"Cody got a goal and he only played five minutes in the first game," Kenneth said.

"So what are the practices like?" Paulo said.

Cody hesitated. It sounded like Paulo was asking him. "We've only had one with Trevor... we had others with the first coach, of course . . . Henry . . . Trevor's our second . . . coach, that is."

Kenneth cut in. "He's a fitness nut, that's for sure. Last practice he ran us into the ground."

"My dad says you win games with your legs and your brain," Paulo said.

Cody almost laughed out loud. His mom always said the same thing to him.

"Take a knee, everyone," Trevor said, as the players gathered around. "Let me first introduce Paulo. He's trying out for the team. Cody invited him. So let's make him welcome — and good luck, Paulo."

Cody didn't like the sound of the murmuring amongst the players. Once they saw him play he figured they'd change their minds pretty quickly, so he decided not to worry.

"Trev, if I may," Ian broke in. "I didn't actually know about this tryout. I've been working on filling the extra spot, to tell you the truth . . ."

"Yeah. We've been working on that," Mitch said.

The Dragons crowded behind Ian and Mitch.

"Maybe we could talk about this for a few minutes before practice," Ian said, his eyebrows raised. He pointed to the parking lot.

Cody thought Ian looked really uncomfortable. Not Trevor, though. He looked more irritated than anything. "I apologize for not giving you notice," he said in an even tone. "No matter. We'll see how it goes and we can discuss it *after* practice."

Ian's gaze wavered, and then lowered to the ground.

"Can I have you and Mitch as line judges again?" Trevor said. "You did a great job last practice. Thanks. And as for you other fellows, I'd really like to emphasize how important it is for you to stay on the sidelines during a practice. I really need you to do that. I can't have interruptions. Okay?"

The three Dragons stared, first at Trevor, and then over at Ian.

"We kinda run the team, Trevor. I'm the sponsor and we like to be involved," Ian said.

"I get ya. And I welcome your involvement, just not during practice. That's my time. Okay? So can I get you on the sidelines with the other parents, and Ian and Mitch pick a sideline. Thanks."

He turned his back on them and the five Dragons walked away, their heads close together.

"Don't forget — I need one of you on the far sideline," Trevor called out.

Mitch broke off and jogged the other way. When they were off the pitch, Trevor dug a piece of crumpled paper from his pocket. "I've taken the liberty of dividing you into two groups," he announced. "I want to scrimmage for thirty minutes, then we'll focus on some skills. We should have a bit of time for fitness, too," he added wryly.

Kenneth looked over meaningfully at Cody.

Cody understood. Another scrimmage? Did that mean Trevor hadn't picked the starters yet? Did that mean the Super Subs still had a chance?

"Give me Cody, Paulo, Kenneth, Timothy, Brandon, Jordan, William, Michael, and Luca at the north end. You're Team A. On the other side, we've got John, Anthony, Tyler, Austin, Nathan, Antonio, Ryan, and Jacob. David, you play with Team B for now. Team B, head to your end and I'll organize you in a sec."

Cody heard more than a few grumbles from the B squad. Paulo tugged on his shirt. "This is not a happy team," he whispered.

Cody noticed Ian had crept back onto the pitch.

Trevor folded his paper and stuffed it back into his pocket. "All the players on my team will play, so let's lighten up a touch," he said. No one responded. Trevor scratched his cheek, his jaw shifting to one side. "Might have to work on that . . ." Cody and his teammates remained silent. "Anyway, Cody and Paulo will be up front, with Brandon, Kenneth, and Jacob across the middle, and the back row will be Timothy, William, Michael, and Luca.

"And I mean it — let's have some fun."

Without warning, Timothy yelled, "I ain't no defender!" He looked ready to explode. "I'm the striker on this team. Didn't Henry tell you anything? I led the league in scoring last year, and now I'm a stupid defender? That's bogus."

He pointed at Paulo. "And what's the deal with him?"

Trevor folded his arms slowly. "I appreciate that it's hard to change positions. But I feel that your skills are better suited to the back row. You're fast, you play hard, and you can kick the ball far. Trust me. You could be one of the best defenders in the league if you put your mind to it."

Timothy's face was almost as red as his hair.

Ian was walking toward his son. "What's wrong, Timmer?" he asked cautiously.

"He wants to stuff me back on defence. You said he knew something about soccer."

Ian's mouth dropped open. "A defender? For real? Trevor, have you lost your mind?"

"I thought I told you to be line judge," Trevor said, his eyes cold and hard. Then his face relaxed, and he smiled. "Anyway, it's just for this practice. I'm trying out a few new things. Not a big deal. If you would . . ."

"I ain't playing defence. No way," Timothy barked. "And I don't get why some new kid gets my spot without even one practice. I mean, who is he?"

Trevor cupped his hands around his mouth and he shouted, "Ryan, come over here." He nodded toward Team B. "Timothy, you play striker for that side. Show me what you've got."

"John and me will fill the net. Count on it," Timothy said, with a cocky grin.

"I'll play with Team B, too," Michael said.

Trevor stared at him, but only for a moment. "Okay, you head on over with Timothy," he said. Trevor then set off toward Team B.

"Go hard, Timmer," Ian said. He slapped his son on the back before heading to the sidelines.

When Trevor and Ian were far enough away not to hear, Timothy looked over at Cody and said in a high-pitched voice, "Humpty Dumpty's gonna have a big fall, and all the Super Subs ain't never gonna put him back together again."

Michael laughed.

"Give it a rest," Kenneth said.

"Don't have to, Super Sub," Timothy sneered. "And I still don't know why you're here," he said to Paulo.

"I came to take your position," Paulo said sweetly.

"Yeah? I came to kick your butt back to your own country, wherever that is," he muttered before he and Michael left.

Kenneth, Luca, Cody, and Paulo grouped together. "This is our chance," Kenneth said excitedly. "We'll have fun by making the starting lineup for the tournament this Friday."

"Sounds good to me," Luca said.

"I'm ready. That Timothy talks too much," Paulo said.

"It'll be fun to shut him up, too," Kenneth said.

Cody kept quiet. He was so nervous he could throw up ten times over. Maybe soccer was fun — of course it was. But somehow this was about more than soccer. This was more important than anything in his life. He couldn't be a Super Sub for the rest of the season, and he wasn't going to quit because of some bullies.

This time the story would end differently.

Humpty Dumpty wasn't going to fall.

Humpty Dumpty was going to score some goals.

15

Timothy shot an icy stare at Cody and Paulo, and slid the ball to John for the kickoff. He one-timed it back to Anthony. Paulo pressured and Anthony swung it wide to Tyler. He had lots of room down the sideline, but Cody noticed he wasn't looking upfield, but rather at Timothy, who was camped out about ten metres past the midfield line.

Cody bolted over and arrived at the same time as the ball. Timothy managed to get a foot on it, but Cody took it away easily.

"Cody!"

Cody passed it square to Kenneth, who took a few steps forward and rifled it to the right side to Jordan. Paulo wasted no time getting into the game. He cut into a gap about ten metres inside Team B's end, and Jordan gave it to him. Cody had so much confidence in Paulo's skills he didn't bother watching, but instead sprinted upfield at an angle toward the sidelines.

Paulo didn't disappoint him. When Anthony tried to challenge, Paulo chipped the ball over his head, allowing Cody to run onto it without breaking stride.

"Cody, again."

Cody crossed it back inside to Kenneth, and then continued on in full flight, with Antonio and Nathan backpedalling furiously. Kenneth rewarded his efforts with a perfect pass onto his right foot at the top of the box. He had a good shot with only Austin between him and the goal, but it was his right foot . . .

Out of the corner of his eye he saw Paulo on the overlap. He delayed, to suck Austin in close, and then slid the ball softly to his new friend. Again, Paulo didn't disappoint. He curved past Austin as if he were a goal post, faked going across the crease, and punched it past David with his left foot on the short side.

"Goooaaallll," Kenneth bellowed.

Cody was too stoked to say anything. He pounded Paulo across the shoulders over and over. Paulo didn't seem to mind. He was just as excited.

"I didn't think the first goal would take so long," Kenneth said, joining the celebration, "but I'll take it."

"Good teamwork," Paulo said.

Luca came bounding up field. "Sweet passing, boys," he said. "I had fun watching that. We relax when it's ten-nothing."

They passed Timothy for the kickoff.

"The little girls get one goal and now they're all giggly," Timothy said.

They ignored him, but when Timothy was out of earshot, Kenneth said, "I'll be giggling even more when he and John are the new Super Subs."

"I'll be hysterical when Timothy's president of the book club," Luca added.

"Nice run, Cody," Jordan said, as they set up for the kickoff. "And great goal . . . other striker." He laughed. "Sorry, what's your name again?"

"Paulo," he said, good-naturedly.

"Paulo! Sorry. Well, awesome goal. Let's get another."

"Way to go, Cody. Way to go, Paulo," William yelled from the back.

"Let's keep it up, boys," Ryan said.

Paulo flashed Cody a thumbs-up. Cody crouched in readiness. He didn't need any encouragement. That was the most fun he'd had all season.

Like before, Timothy took the kickoff and gave it to John, who passed to Anthony. He held it for a bit, and then passed it back to Antonio. The ball ping-ponged among the back line as Cody and Paulo waited, not wanting to get beat with one pass. Finally, Antonio decided to press matters and rolled a pass to the right to Austin.

Cody knew Austin wasn't the best ball handler. All he ever really did was boot the ball downfield. Cody left his position and pressed forward. Austin saw him coming and swerved outside, his head down. About three metres from the sideline, Austin planted his left foot and reared back with his right. Cody closed in and jumped across Austin, holding out his left foot. His toe was able to drag across the top of the ball just as Austin was about to kick, enough to nudge it closer to the sideline.

Austin missed it and fell down. Cody hoped over him, trapped the ball with his right foot, and immediately set off down the sideline. He was surprised to see Paulo to the inside, slightly ahead of him. It was amazing how Paulo always seemed to be near the ball, even though he wasn't the fastest runner. Cody passed it — and then groaned.

He hadn't noticed Anthony, who was right on him. Paulo stepped over the ball with his right foot and with a slight nudge from his left foot let it roll up the back of his right calf. He took a half step, whipping his right heel up. The ball flew over Anthony's head.

Cody wanted to cheer, it was such an amazing move. Paulo cut to his left to avoid colliding with Anthony. Cody's fellow Super Sub wasn't going to let that happen, however. He lowered his shoulder and ploughed into Paulo, knocking him clear off his feet.

The whistle blasted.

"Foul. Direct kick."

Trevor raced over. He looked mad.

"That would be a red card in a game," he said.

Anthony shrugged and looked away. Paulo got to his feet slowly and dusted off his shirt.

"Are you okay?" Cody asked Paulo.

Paulo flashed a grin. "No problem. It tickled."

"I won't tolerate that kind of play," Trevor continued with Anthony. "Do you hear me?"

"Sorry," he muttered.

"Say it to Paulo," Trevor ordered.

Anthony looked off to the side. "Sorry."

Trevor rubbed his chin really hard several times. "Free kick Team A. Line up."

Paulo placed the ball on the spot of the foul. "When I kick, run to the far post," he whispered to Cody.

Jordan usually took the free kicks for the Lions, but after that hard foul even he didn't say anything when Paulo set up to take it. Cody stationed himself on the far side with the defenders. David had been busy organizing a wall about twenty-four metres out, but he broke off when he saw Cody. "Someone mark Cody over there," he shouted suddenly.

"Like I'm worried about Egg-Head," Tyler said, loud enough for everyone to hear.

Cody's stomach tightened and an uncomfortable tingling travelled down his back. The dis hurt, but at least no one bothered to mark him. Paulo took two short steps and sent a hard left-footed cross that sailed over the wall and curled to the far post, just like he'd said.

It was one of the easiest goals Cody had ever scored. David had no chance to stop Cody's header, and the ball flew into the net, about half a metre inside the post. David threw his hands in the air. "Great marking, guys," he said.

Cody felt sorry for the goaltender. Tough to have two goals scored so quickly. "I'll get the ball for ya," Cody said, and he ran to retrieve it.

"Thanks," David said, as Cody threw it to him. "Now will you stop scoring on me?" He said it funny, so Cody knew he was joking.

"No one covered me. It was lucky."

"That new kid sure can play," David said.

"He's part soccer player, part magician," Cody said.

"He should take those fancy moves back where he came from," Anthony said. He stood glaring at Cody and looked ready to kill someone.

David rolled his eyes and threw the ball toward midfield.

"What? He's . . . he's a good player," Cody said.

"We've got enough good players from *this* country," Anthony fumed. "We don't need foreigners taking over."

"Taking over what? He's just trying out."

Anthony wasn't interested in explaining himself. "It's bogus," he said simply. "His kind ain't welcome, period."

"What kind are you talking about?"

"The brown banana kind," Timothy interjected. Tyler and John snickered.

"And tell his dad to get a job," Anthony said.

"He has a job," Cody answered, bewildered by Anthony's attitude. "He's a doctor at the hospital."

"Tell Jungle Boy I'll break his legs if he tries one of those chicken moves on me," Antonio said.

Anthony, Timothy, Tyler, Antonio, and John stood in front of Cody. He took a step back.

A loud whistle blasted. "Line up for the kickoff," Trevor said, pushing past the wall of Team B players. "What's the problem here?"

Timothy didn't say anything. The others took their cue from him and turned away. Cody jogged back to his end. Kenneth and Luca were waiting for him near midfield.

"That didn't look too friendly," Kenneth said.

"No big deal," Cody said. He didn't want to tell Kenneth what Anthony had said; they'd been friends for a long time. Besides, he didn't understand it. He got that guys would bully him because of his bald head. But what had Paulo done? What was this garbage about his skin colour?

Paulo held out his fist, and Cory gave it an uneasy bump.

"Told ya to watch the outside post," Paulo said.

"Sweet kick. Total gift goal."

"You were in the right spot, and the header was cool to watch. You and I are a good team. We'll get those ten goals, no problem."

As things turned out, Paulo wasn't that far off. By the time Trevor called the scrimmage, Team A had counted another four goals, two of them by Cody. Paulo and Kenneth always seemed to have the ball on their feet, and the Team A players passed it around seemingly at will.

"Gather around, boys, and take a knee," Trevor said. Cody noticed the Dragons creeping onto the pitch. "That wasn't too bad. Conditioning is still a concern — we aren't ready to run for ninety minutes. Ball skills are good, though, and some of you seem to almost know what you're doing."

He paused. "That was a joke, by the way." He paused again. "You're gonna make me work for it, aren't you? Tough crowd." He sighed. "We don't have a practice between now and our first tournament game on Friday, so I want to work on some positioning with our starting lineup. Before I call out the names I want you to remember that all of you will play, that's a promise. And just because you're starting doesn't mean you stay a starter for the rest of the season. The hardest-working players get the playing time."

Cody could hardly breathe.

"We'll have David in goal."

A few guys laughed.

"Defenders are Luca, William, Jacob, and Michael."

Cody was happy for Luca. He'd played solid defence during the scrimmage and totally deserved it.

"At midfield I want Brandon, Tyler, and Kenneth."

Cody's heart jumped at Kenneth's name. Three Super Subs were in. What about him?

"For strikers, we'll go with Jordan, Paulo, and Cody."

Timothy gasped, and John's eyes bugged way out.

"That's if Paulo accepts the invitation to play with us," Trevor continued.

Paulo flicked his eyebrows. "Sounds good, Coach," he said.

Trevor nodded. "As you kids say, that is totally awesome." He cleared his throat. "Those not starting, can you fire some balls at David at the far end? I want to run through some formations with the starters to make sure we're all on the same page come Friday."

No sooner had he finished than the Dragons surrounded him. Cody noticed some of the other parents standing in a larger group on the sidelines. One of the parents, who he thought was Kenneth's father, was nodding his head rapidly and gesturing emphatically with his hands; several times he pointed at the Dragons. Cody could only wonder what they were talking about. As for the Dragons, there was little doubt what was on their minds.

"Timothy led the league in scoring. I mean, what's going through your head?" Cody heard Ian say. "He's got

European scouts interested. I've lined up a tournament in Florida so they can see him. I didn't invest all this money in this team for him to sit. That's unacceptable."

"Hey, Cody. Come over here," Kenneth said.

Kenneth was with Luca and Paulo. Cody would've liked to hear more, but he went over to be polite.

"This ain't the end," Kenneth said. "We haven't done anything, not yet, anyway. Friday's game is totally huge. We gotta play fierce — or we'll be Super Subs again before we can say . . . before we can say . . . Timothy's a loser!"

"I can say that pretty quick," Luca said.

"Ain't that the truth," Kenneth said. He held out his fist. Cody felt silly, but he bumped it along with the others.

The Dragons were still giving Trevor a hard time, and every once in awhile Cody heard a raised voice.

"Not fair."

"Outsider . . ."

"We paid good money . . ."

"Foreigner . . ."

"Let's kick the ball around until Trevor's finished with his meeting," Kenneth said, leading them away. Soon they were playing an intense game of keep-away. William and Jacob joined in, as did Jordan and Brandon, and finally David. The memory of Anthony's dissing, the bullying, and the Dragons drifted away as Cody raced around trying to get the ball.

16

Cody leaned over and grabbed the bottom of his shorts, gasping for air. He felt like he'd run a marathon. And what did he have to show for it? Nothing but three shots and a bunch of near misses. The Rangers had kept six or seven defenders behind midfield for practically the entire game to form an impenetrable wall in front of their goalie. Their midfielders moved up only for corners and free kicks. The good news was the score was still 0–0. The Lions had a chance to win their first game this season, and in a tourna ment no less.

Paulo stood about twelve metres to his right. Unlike him, Paulo didn't seem tired at all, and he'd been play-ing great. The Rangers goalie bounced the ball twice, and then gave his left winger a quick look. Cody figured the ball was going to him. Apparently, Paulo thought the same, and they both broke as the goalie booted it.

Their hunch was right. The ball caromed in a line drive toward the sidelines. Cody jumped, his leg protesting at the effort so late in the game. The Ranger winger challenged, but he'd reacted a bit late, and Cody had a clear header.

"Yo, Cody! Left!"

The crafty forward had backed off once he'd seen Cody get position. Cody knocked the ball down to him. Paulo flicked it on with the outside of his left foot and motored toward the Rangers' goal. Cody landed awkwardly and his knee jammed a bit. He jogged along the sidelines tentatively to test it out. As usual, a whack of Rangers were defending. Paulo was drifting outside, dragging the ball with his instep. Kenneth was putting in an effort to support, and Jordan was overlapping on the left wing.

His knee still hurt and Cody groaned as he forced himself into support as well. It was torture and he almost wished the game would end. A shout from the sidelines caught his attention.

"The guy is useless — done nothing all game."

"Get off the pitch, Humpty."

He looked over. Timothy and John were laughing at him.

"You wanna borrow some of my hair, Cue-Ball?" Tyler added.

Great teammates! He took off to the far side, ignoring his searing lungs and throbbing knee. He needed to run. He needed to prove something.

"Turn and face," Kenneth gasped as Cody whipped by.

Cody did just in time to see Paulo, who had his back to two defenders, suddenly whirl, slip the ball between a defender's legs, and jump past them both. Kenneth and Brandon came over to support up the middle. Jordan was still wide left. Cody decided to leave the supporting to the two midfielders and stayed to the left also. The Rangers defenders shifted across to cut Paulo off from the goal, and that left a sole Rangers defender to mark two Lions forwards.

Could Paulo work some more magic?

Yes!

At the top of the box, he faked a pass back to Kenneth, stepped over the ball with his inside foot, faked to the outside, then did a 360-degree spin, curling around the left shoulder of a defender, all the time keeping the ball cradled with his right foot. Cody didn't waste time watching. Trusting in his friend's wizardry, he broke free and stormed the box hoping for a rebound when Paulo shot.

But Paulo wasn't done. Instead of taking the bad-angle shot, he twisted his body and lofted a cross. Without thinking Cody threw his left foot at the ball. The goalie threw himself headlong as well, and they collided about four metres from the line. The goalie's elbow whacked Cody in the cheek and his shoulder crashed into his ribs. It was a jumble of arms and legs, with dirt everywhere and the goalie right on top of Cody. He heard a roar from the spectators, and then felt someone pull him to his feet.

"Total commitment. Beyond awesome."

That was Kenneth. What was he talking about?

Then Paulo came running over and pounded Cody on

the back. "I knew it. I just knew you'd be there. Didn't see you, but I knew it."

Cody stared at them both, dazed.

Kenneth laughed and clapped his hands together. "You scored, dummy," he said. "Be happy."

"I didn't think I touched the ball," Cody said, still having trouble believing it.

"Then I'll take the goal," Kenneth joked.

Jordan, Brandon, Luca, and William joined them and they slapped one another's backs and high-fived.

The Rangers wasted no time kicking off. The ball went wide left, and Cody went over to pressure. His knee still hurt, but somehow the goal had taken the pain away. The Rangers reversed the ball to the right wing but Paulo was there to force it back. And that's the way it went for the next ten minutes. Energized by their goal, the Lions were a touch quicker to the ball and able to keep it out of their end.

The Rangers' right back had the ball and, Cody was moving forward to press when he heard the whistle blow. Cody swung around, figuring someone had committed a foul away from the ball, which was irritating considering the score was so close. Kenneth put an arm around his neck.

"Not bad for a bunch of Super Subs," he said.

Again, Cody didn't know what he was talking about.

Kenneth shook his head and chuckled. "First win of the year, bro."

"We won?" Cody said.

"That's what happens when the game is over and we have more goals than the other team," Kenneth said.

"I guess I lost track of time."

"You scare me sometimes," Kenneth laughed, "but you did score the winner, so I'll cut you some slack."

Their teammates crowded around. "That was a sweet goal," William declared, cuffing Paulo and Cody around the shoulders.

"I was so tired all I could do was watch," Brandon said.

"I had a clear view. Cody went total animal on that goal — and Paulo . . ." Jordan shook his head and whistled softly.

As a group, they shuffled to the sidelines, where Trevor greeted them by clapping. He didn't let up until they were all off the pitch. "How about that, lads? You fought for it. Fought hard. Good patience and good work ethic," he enthused.

Jacob came over to Cody. "Beautiful goal," he said. Jacob was a quiet kid; Cody couldn't remember the last time the midfielder had said anything to him, so the compliment meant a lot.

He was about to compliment Jacob back when he felt a hand on his shoulder.

"Are you okay, dear?"

His mom peered at him closely. Jacob backed away.

Cody dipped his shoulder and pulled back. "I'm fine," he said.

"Let me see. Did you hit your head?"

"No."

A few players looked over.

Cody turned crimson. He glared at his mom.

Suddenly, she laughed and patted him on the shoulder

139

again. "Just teasing. That was an exciting game. Really marvellous."

Cody nodded, relieved that she had stopped going on about him being hurt. "Thanks. Everyone played great."

"I'll wait for you over by the parking lot," she said quickly.

Trevor called them over. "I'm proud of you lads for hanging in there and not losing your cool." He looked totally stoked. "Tough to score against a team that packs the back line. So give yourselves a cheer." He began to clap again — alone. Trevor looked around, and then laughed. "I forgot what a tough crowd you are. You just won your first game of the season. Enjoy it. Now give me a moment. I have to speak to the tournament organizer for a second." He ran off.

"Whoopee," Timothy said. "We get a lucky goal and our coach goes mental. Give me a break."

"No such thing as a lucky goal," Paulo said. "They all count."

"Like I need a soccer lesson from you," Timothy said. "You're not even on the team."

"For a guy not on the team he sure played a lot," Kenneth said.

"And I didn't ask for your opinion, either, goofball," Timothy said.

Kenneth pretended to be surprised. "That's weird. I thought you did."

"A funny man who's not funny," John said.

"Did you enjoy watching the game?" Paulo said.

"And watching us actually win?" Kenneth said.

Cody listened in awe. They were fearless. He was afraid to even talk to Timothy.

Timothy's fists were balled tightly. "Dad, do we need these two clowns on the team? They're a joke."

Ian had been huddled with the Dragons. They all came over.

"I ain't sitting on the bench for Egg-Head," John said.

"No. You're sitting for a real soccer player," Paulo said.

"Says you," Timothy shot back, and he shoved Paulo in the chest.

"Hold on, there . . . whatever your name is," Ian said. He pointed a finger at Paulo. "I figured you for a trouble-maker the second I laid eyes on you."

"Total troublemaker," Mitch said.

"Never wanted him on the team to begin with," Antonio's father said, with a firm jerk of his hat.

"I didn't expect you to be mixed up with this, Kenneth," Ian said. "But I can't have a bad seed on the team. You and Paulo will have to hand in your uniforms. I'll even refund half your fee as a goodwill gesture — can't do more than that."

"Totally fair," Mitch said.

Cody's head whirled. Kenneth and Paulo kicked off the team, and just after their first win? It was ridiculous. What was he going to do without them?

"I ain't playing if they're off the team," Luca said, "so you can have my uniform, too."

"Like that's such a big deal," Antonio said. "Big pile of dog poo on the pitch is all you are."

Kenneth's face had gone pale. Cody knew Kenneth loved soccer as much as he did. Luca also looked upset.

Paulo looked plain angry. They'd defended him, and now they were taking the heat. That was plain wrong.

"No one needs to be kicked off the team," Cody said to Ian. "I'll leave; that's what you want, anyway. Everyone else can play."

He forced himself to take a breath, not quite believing what he'd said. He felt good about it, though. Soccer was done and that sucked, but those three guys meant a lot to him, and he wasn't going to let them down.

"As you wish," Ian said.

"Never should've listened to Henry about him," Antonio's dad said.

Mitch nodded vigorously.

"Now he has time to grow some curls," Timothy said. John and Antonio smirked, and Tyler pretended to brush his hair.

"Can someone fill me in on what's going on?" Trevor's hands were on his hips, his eyes narrowed and focused on Ian.

"I had to deal with a little discipline issue, to take care of some bad seeds on this team and gain control of a situation before it got out of control," Ian said. "Kenneth and Paulo were mouthing off, being rude to a teammate, and Paulo even used physical force, which I simply cannot tolerate. I asked him to leave, and Kenneth, too; and then Luca and Egg . . . I mean Cody, said they wanted to quit, too."

Trevor didn't respond right away. He rubbed his chin with his right hand very slowly. "Are you accusing Paulo of hitting a teammate?" he said point-blank to Ian.

Ian rolled his neck and shrugged. "I know what I saw."

"Answer the question," Trevor said.

"Are you telling me what to do?" Ian said.

The other parents had gathered behind the Dragons in a tight semi-circle. He spotted his mom in the back.

"I'm asking you a simple question. Did you see Paulo hit a teammate?" Trevor said.

"Yes, I did," Ian said.

"He's lying," Cody shouted. "Timothy pushed Paulo. Ian's lying."

"Don't talk to me like that, you little . . ." Ian said.

"Watch yourself," Trevor said. "I think you're forgetting who's the adult and who's the kid."

Ian shrugged again and tugged on his hat. "I think you're forgetting who owns this team."

"We didn't know it was your team," Kenneth's dad called out.

Ian whirled around. "Haven't you noticed who's been paying for all this? Do you think track pants and hats and bags and buses for tournaments grow on trees? Do you? Well, they don't."

"They sure don't," Mitch said.

"So let's not waste any more time taking about whose team it is," Ian said, "and we don't need to waste more time talking about these boys. I want them off the team, so that's the way it is. You don't like it, you can pull your boys, too. I don't care. I've got dozens of players dying to get on this team."

"No problem attracting talent," Mitch said.

"We don't need 'em, anyway," Antonio's dad said.

The two other Dragons looked very pleased.

Trevor's eyes had a faraway look. "This has been a very uncomfortable moment for all of us; I think we can agree on that," he said finally. The parents quieted down, and the players turned to listen. "I do agree with Ian about one thing. There definitely are bad seeds on this team, probably about five bad seeds, and they're wearing what can only be described as the most ridiculous hats I've ever seen in my life."

Cody caught himself from laughing by covering his mouth with his hand. He hadn't expected that.

"Moreover, I don't agree that this is your team," Trevor said. "The boys own this team, and no one asked you for the bus or the bags or anything. You can't stop the Lions from playing tomorrow morning at nine o'clock any more than I can stop the sun from rising."

"You think so?" Ian said. "Well, how are you gonna play when Timothy is off the team?"

"And John," Mitch said.

"And Antonio," his dad said.

"And Tyler."

"And Nathan."

"And Michael."

"We'll play even better," Kenneth said.

"Like we did today," Luca said.

Ian ignored them. "Trevor, let's say this simply didn't work out," he said in a friendly tone. "No need for more unpleasantness. I can manage the team fine, so thanks for your efforts and now it's time for you to leave."

"Don't we get a say in this?" Kenneth said.

"We should vote," Luca said.

"You should get a life," Timothy said.

"Kenneth, I like your idea," Trevor said. "The players should decide."

"Kids don't decide these things," Ian sputtered.

"I say they do," Trevor replied. "Lions, there you have it. If you want me to coach, hold up your hand."

Kenneth's hand was up in a flash, along with Luca's and David's. Cody saw William, Ryan, and Paulo, and then Jordan, Brandan, Jacob, and Austin follow suit. Cody raised his hand.

Kenneth was watching Anthony. He kept his arms firmly to his sides.

"That would appear to be a clear majority," Trevor said.

"This is not going to happen," Ian shrieked. "You can't just take over my team. I'm the manager. I'm the sponsor. I won't allow it."

"And I ain't sitting on the bench behind Chicken-Leg and Banana-Boy," Timothy said.

"You can shut up," Paulo said, his eyes blazing.

"You shouldn't be on this team," Antonio yelled at Paulo.

Paulo dismissed them with a backhanded wave.

"What's up with you?" Kenneth said to Anthony. "When did you go over to the dark side?"

"When did you become a foreigner-lover?" Anthony's face was beet-red, and he looked so angry he could literally burst apart. "My dad lost his job because foreigners will work for cheap. I'm not playing with him."

"So don't," Luca said.

"Good idea," Anthony snapped, and he stomped off. His father stared long and hard at Trevor, and then followed his son without a word.

"Dad, do something," Timothy demanded.

"This has gotten out of control," Ian said in a shaky voice. "I need you to leave and let me . . ."

"That's not going to happen," Trevor said. He studied the boys crowded around Timothy. "I understand young boys say and do things in the heat of the moment. I'm a big believer in second chances. You can still be part of this team, but you need to apologize for your comments and behaviour, and then you need to agree to work hard and try to help the team win. I know you can play, but you all have a sense of entitlement, which means you think you can do whatever you want without consequences. I don't blame you for that. It's the Dragons who are to blame. But you need to learn to respect the game, and that starts with respecting your teammates. I'm willing to forget what's happened and move forward, but . . ."

"No way I play with this jerk," Timothy interrupted, looking at his dad. "Find me another team. Come on, guys. Are you gonna play with this bunch of losers?"

Evidently, they weren't. Timothy and John led the way, followed by Tyler, Antonio, Michael, and Nathan. Antonio turned and pointed at Paulo and Cody. "We'll find other teams, and when we play the Lions you two won't walk off the pitch."

Cody felt his energy slip away. This was crazy. The season was over. They had no players.

Trevor shrugged and crossed his arms. "Good. Bad attitudes are gone. I'd rather finish this tournament with . . ." a big smile crossed his face, "eleven good men than have bullies and close-minded boys tearing a team apart." He looked around at the remaining parents. "Are we good?"

Most flashed a thumbs-up, and a few chorused "Sure" and "Let's do it, Coach."

Cody quickly counted the remaining players: eleven! Trevor was right. It was enough to field a team, although they wouldn't have any subs.

"What about it, boys?" Trevor said.

"I'm liking it big-time," Kenneth said.

"Darn right," Luca sounded.

"Best team we've had all year," David said.

Paulo came up to Cody. "You and me, we're gonna score some goals tomorrow."

Cody felt a fire burning in his chest. "We're going to do more than that. We're going to win this tournament," he said.

The players and the parents began chanting: "*Li-ons, Li-ons, Li-ons!*"

17

Cody flew toward the penalty area and took Paulo's pass without breaking stride. His confidence sky-high after scoring earlier in the first half off a sweet feed from Paulo, Cody faked an outside move on the Flames' midfielder and cut hard to his left, leaping into the air at the same time. The midfielder had over-committed, and he threw his right knee outward in a desperate attempt to slow Cody down.

Cody crumpled to the ground. The whistle stopped play, and a cheer went up from the Lions parents in anticipation of the free kick.

"Awesome move," Kenneth said, running over to help him up.

Cody remained on the ground. The midfielder's knee had gone straight into his thigh.

"Yo, Cody. You okay?" he heard Paulo ask.

Cody rolled onto his back and pulled his leg into his chest.

"I think he's really hurt," Kenneth said.

"But we've got no subs," Brandon said.

"At least the kid got a yellow card," Jordan said.

"Great, and we go down a player," Brandon said.

By this time Trevor and Leandro had come over.

"Where'd you get hit, son?" Trevor asked calmly.

Cody pointed to his leg.

"Can you straighten it out?" Leandro said.

Cody tried, and a rush of pain swept down his leg. He shook his head.

"I think you're down to ten players," Leandro said to Trevor. "It doesn't appear that he can play."

Cody opened his eyes and saw the disappointment in Kenneth's face. Even Paulo looked downcast. He began his breathing, just like Dr. Charya had taught him, and slowly the pain seeped away.

Leandro lowered himself close to the ground and whispered in Cody's ear, "Do you think you can get up or do we need to carry you off?"

"Help me stand up, please," Cody said.

Leandro and Trevor hooked their hands under his arms and pulled him to his feet.

"I assume you're sending in a sub?" the referee said to Trevor.

"We don't have any," Trevor said.

"But I'm not going off," Cody announced.

The referee looked at Trevor. "He has to go off until the next stoppage; then he can come back on."

Cody gritted his teeth. "I'll be fine. It's a charley horse. It'll go away when I run around." He wasn't going to let his teammates down — no way!

"Are you sure? No one is going to criticize you. That was a bad foul," Leandro said, and then he turned to the referee and added, "and it should have been a red card."

The referee grimaced. "Make a decision, please. Is he playing?"

Cody nodded emphatically. Trevor grinned and slapped him on the back. Cody forced himself to walk as normally as possible. The spectators gave him a nice round of applause, and the referee whistled play to resume. Paulo flashed him a thumbs-up and ran downfield. Jordan placed the ball for the free kick.

"You're playing great," Trevor told him. "Keep attacking, especially the right back. He doesn't have much outside speed. Now keep warm because you're back out there as soon as we get another stoppage."

Cody nodded. He wasn't so sure about his own speed. But one thing was certain. With no subs, he had to play. His dad caught his eye. He nodded to him, and his dad nodded back. Usually his dad read a newspaper or a book during a game, or he waited in the car. Maybe he was starting to like soccer, even a bit?

Cody felt his leg again. It was aching, and he could feel it tightening up already. So he had to play — but could he?

★★★

Deep in the second half and still playing, Cody rubbed his leg to loosen it up. He figured they were close to injury time, and maybe even in it. The tension was overwhelming as the Lions clung to their one-goal lead. Cody could run, but it was awkward. The Flames' goaltender placed the ball down on the six-yard marker and got ready to kick. Cody assessed the situation quickly. His teammates had done an awesome job picking up the slack for him. Paulo was bent over catching his breath. The midfielders had played like madmen, especially Kenneth, whose shirt had turned a darker shade of blue with all the sweat. Luca and William had formed an effective wall in front of David. And of course, the Lions goalie had been his usual spectacular self.

Cody summoned every last bit of energy and will, and, ignoring the pain, bent over to stretch out his leg. That was enough of Dr. Charya's breathing technique and limping around. These guys needed him to play. The Flames' netminder tended to kick to his wingers. As he approached the ball for the goal kick, Cody raced over to his left as fast as his injured leg could carry him.

The ball came right toward him. Cody cut in front of the winger and headed the ball to Paulo. The Lions' supporters cheered, and Paulo corralled the bouncing ball at the forty and curled into the middle of the pitch.

"Nice play, Cody," Trevor shouted.

That was the first compliment since his injury, which made sense because it was the first time he'd done anything. He took off parallel to Paulo, about ten metres further downfield.

Paulo punched it over to him, as if grateful to let

someone else dribble. Cody continued along the left side. He had two choices: attack the goal or delay and wait for support. He had a split second to decide because a defender was charging right at him. A quick glance back made the decision easy. No one was running up except Paulo, who was hoofing it up the middle. Their teammates were simply too tired.

Cody would have to try something alone. He waited until the defender was two metres away. Then he flicked the ball onward with the outside of his left foot and sped after it. The leg throbbed, but the pain somehow spurred him on rather than slowing him down.

Cody pulled away and swept toward the goal, as another defender raced over to cut him off. The goalie also came out, which didn't leave much net to shoot at. Maybe he could sneak it inside the post?

"Yo, Cody."

Without looking, Cody slid on his right thigh and swung his left foot, slicing the ball just over the goalie's fingertips.

Paulo met the ball gracefully with a half volley, directing it into the net. A huge roar rose from the sidelines.

"Yea, Lions."

"Beautiful goal. Go, Lions, go."

"Great job, Lions."

Once again a pair of hands reached under his arms and hoisted him to his feet. His helper added a few not-so-gentle pats on his back.

"I'm gonna call you The Postman — cause you always deliver," Kenneth shouted.

Paulo came over, his huge grin pasted across his face. "I didn't think you heard me," he said.

Soon the entire team was celebrating, until the referee finally yelled, "Line it up, Lions. Game's not over."

Kenneth said loudly, "Yes it is, Mr. Referee, sir."

Cody's leg hurt too much to laugh. He hobbled after his teammates to centre, praying the game would end soon. The Flames barely had time to kick off when Cody heard the most awesome sound any tired group of players can hear when they're winning — the whistle. The game was over, and the Lions were in the semi-finals. And they'd done it without any subs!

Kenneth was thinking the same thing. He repeated to whoever would listen, "We don't need no Super Subs; we got ourselves the Super Starters."

"You guys were awesome today. I could've read a book back there," David said gleefully.

Cody knew that wasn't true. He'd made some huge saves.

"Nice to win — nice to win," Luca kept saying.

"Huge effort, Lions," Brandon said, as he and his buddy Jordan hugged and high-fived.

"Listen up, lads," Trevor said. "Hold it down a sec." He waited for them to quiet. "That was inspiring. Great soccer; great determination and heart, and no quitting. I loved it." That set off another loud cheer. "I want to give a game ball to someone who paid the price and kept in the game after a tough knock — Cody!"

Cody paid another price as Kenneth put him in a head-lock and Luca pummelled him a few times for fun, and then David and William added their licks. Cody felt himself blush furiously.

"Let's not break his head, too," Trevor joked. "How's the leg holding up?" he asked him.

"It should be okay by this afternoon," Cody replied. It actually didn't feel too bad.

"The next game is at six o'clock on this same pitch. Be here an hour early again. I know it's hard to play two games in one day, but it's equally hard on the other team." He turned to the parents. "Nothing too heavy for lunch, please. Pasta with some chicken is good. I'll see you back shortly — in the semi-finals."

They all cheered at that, too. Cody clapped along. His dad caught his eye and he waved for Cody to follow him to the parking lot. Cody cut between two groups of parents. He heard Kenneth's voice from behind one group and he stopped to listen.

"So let's meet up after lunch," Kenneth said. "I'm way too stoked to sit at home and wait for the game."

"I'm up for it," Luca said.

"Sounds good," Paulo said.

Cody slipped away before they could see him. He felt relieved, although also a bit light-headed. That would have been embarrassing if they'd caught him eavesdropping. He told himself he didn't have the right to be mad at them. Kenneth and Luca were nice guys. He couldn't really say they were friends, though. They just played on the same team, really. Come to think of it, he barely knew them; and he didn't know Paulo, either. It bothered him that Kenneth and Luca had only just met Paulo and they'd invited him, but he was such a cool kid and full of jokes. It made sense. Anyway, it would be better to go home and relax.

Besides, what could he do about it?

As soon as they were in the car and driving home Cody turned on the radio and looked out the window.

His dad turned the radio down. "That was a fun game," he said. "I think Mom will be taking you to the afternoon game, though. I have some work to do."

"Yup," he said.

"You sound a bit down," his dad said. "I figured you'd be excited to win and move on."

"Just tired . . . and my leg hurts."

"That makes sense, after the collision you were in. Once you got up I knew you were okay, but for a second there I got a bit worried. It was a great goal. You made a nice . . . what do you call it . . . a cross kick?"

"It's called a cross, Dad."

He laughed. "Well, it was a beauty of a cross, at least in my opinion."

It suddenly occurred to him that his dad had watched the whole game — or at least most of it. "Too bad you can't see the semis," he said.

The car slowed for a red light. His dad leaned his left elbow on the doorframe and rested his head on his hand. "Now that I think about it, I guess I could work later. We aren't going out tonight."

The light changed.

"If you want," Cody said softly.

"I know I've been working a lot," he said, driving off

again. "And that's been hard on you and Mom." He turned a corner.

Cody kept looking out the window. His dad had apologized for working and missing stuff a hundred times.

His dad swallowed heavily. "I suppose working has been my way of dealing with your . . . with your illness. Maybe Mom has dealt with it by being a bit overprotective. I guess we both dealt with it in our own way. Please believe me when I say that I wanted to be home more, but home always reminded me of you . . . of you getting sick . . . and I simply couldn't handle the thought of you not getting better."

The back of Cody's neck tingled and he felt unsettled in his stomach. His dad had never spoken to him so directly before about his cancer.

"I really admire how well you handled it," his dad continued. "You probably handled it better than me or Mom, to be honest; and to see you back on that field doing so well, that made me proud to be your dad. I just wanted to tell you that."

Cody's chest felt tight. His dad had stopped talking, and he got the feeling he should say something. "Maybe . . . it was harder on you and Mom than on me," he said finally. "All I had to do was get healthy. You and Mom had to worry."

Their eyes met. His dad's eyes were glassy.

"Perhaps you're right," his dad said, "but it's still no excuse." A smile broke out. "And I'm beginning to like this silly game of yours. So, guess what? I'm coming this afternoon and you can't stop me. Go, Lions, go!"

They both laughed, although Cody knew neither of them thought it was really funny.

"Do you mind if I turn up the radio?" Cody asked.

"Sure. Go ahead."

The idea of his mom and dad coming together to the game cheered him up. So what if Kenneth, Luca, and Paulo had left him out? He needed to rest his leg.

A hot bath would help.

That would be the best thing.

A hot bath.

The rubber ball squirted between his fingers. It bounced off the floor and through the railings, and then down the stairs, ricocheting off a window before finally stopping in front of the doorway leading to the kitchen.

"Cody!"

His mom held the ball in her hands.

"Sorry!"

She sighed. "Can you find something else to do other than throw a teeny ball around the house? Besides, I've asked you to stop already — twice."

"Sorry. Only I don't have anything to do."

"You said you were going to take a bath for your leg."

"I did."

"Did you do your stretches?"

"Yeah."

"Why don't you read?"

"I don't have a book."

"You have tons in your room."

"I've read them all."

He heard her take a deep breath. "Why don't you go downstairs? You have a basement full of toys that you never use. Or go outside and get the wiggles out. "

There she went again — treating him like a baby. Thirteen-year-olds didn't have the wiggles. "Can I go to the park and kick the ball around instead?" he said.

"You played this morning and you're playing again in a few hours. Weren't you the kid with the sore leg?"

"It's something to do — and it means I won't bug you," he grinned.

"You've convinced me. But be careful, and no talking to people you don't know, and don't be too long. You should have a snack, and we have to leave at around four-thirty."

"What time is it now?"

"Two."

He put on his shoes.

"Here's a sweatshirt," his mom said.

"I'm fine. It's not cold."

"There's a touch of a chill in the air."

"I'm fine."

"Cody. Put it on, please."

"Mom. I said I don't want it."

"You'll get sick and . . ." She looked quickly at her phone, and then more closely at him. "Okay. Don't blame me if . . ." She paused. "Okay. See you soon. Come home if you get hungry and I'll fix you up a snack."

He pulled his ball out from the closet. "I had a big lunch, but maybe."

She gave him a kiss, and opened the door for him.

"Have fun," she called out when he was halfway down the driveway.

He waved his hand over his head without turning around. As soon as he was on the sidewalk he dropped the ball to the ground and began to dribble. He instantly felt better. This was a good idea. He'd test the leg out and stretch a bit. Soon he began to jog slowly, and at the end of the block he went a little faster. The leg was going to be okay. It would hurt, but he'd been through a whole lot worse than this.

The park came into view. He slowed and peered through the trees to the basketball court, like he always did, to make sure Trane or Stick weren't there. The coast was clear. He faked to his left, did a crossover with his right foot, and then nudging the ball with the outside of his right foot cut hard to his right and straight ahead between two trees — and skidded to a stop. Kenneth, Paulo, and Luca were waving at him.

"Hey! I was worried you didn't get Paulo's email." Kenneth grinned. "Pass for once in your life, wouldja?"

Luca and Paulo laughed. Too stunned to answer, Cody sent a floating left-footer over.

"So, what's shaking, semi-final guy?" Kenneth said.

"Not much," Cody managed.

"I assume you were late because you were doing semi-final stuff," Luca said.

"Sorta."

"That's such a semi-final thing to say," Kenneth said. "You must be on the Lions Football Club. You know . . . the team that won both its tournament games in dramatic fashion."

"I guess I am."

Kenneth made a face. "Actually, we were about to give up on you. Where were you?"

"Yeah, my email said one-thirty," Paulo said.

"You've missed half an hour of me talking about myself," Kenneth said.

"That's thirty minutes of my life I'll never get back," Luca said.

"So, your leg seems okay," Paulo said, pointing.

"He's fine," Kenneth said. "Told you. You are okay, right?" He sounded really worried.

"Can't believe that jerk didn't get a red card. I mean, he injures one of our best players and gets to stay in the game. Totally ridiculous call. He definitely tried to hurt you," Luca said.

Cody's mind was whirling. His mom had kicked him off the computer not long after they got home, which must be why he missed Paulo's email. That meant he'd been invited all along.

"Hey, Cody. You okay?" Kenneth said. "You seemed a bit out of it."

"I'm good. Just a bit tired. I jogged over here and I've been stretching the leg a lot, so . . ." He'd forgotten what he was trying to say.

"I can't tell you guys how stoked I am about the game tonight," Kenneth said. "The season was looking totally grim — and now everything's different."

"Do you guys know who we're gonna play ?" Luca said.

"I checked the website," Kenneth said. "It's the Thornhill Storm. They're third in our league, so it'll be a tough one. They beat us 3–0 last time we played, but then again we didn't have the Super Subs . . . plus one." Kenneth held his hands out to Paulo, and he bowed, grinning broadly. "I also checked out their stats," Kenneth continued. "They're a pretty solid defensive team. They've scored fourteen goals in eight league games, but have only given up six against, and three of those were against United."

"Are you sure it's the Thornhill Storm?" Luca said.

Kenneth nodded.

"Then I know something you don't," Luca said.

Kenneth looked stunned. "That's . . . But that's impossible. You don't know anything. Everyone knows that."

"That may be true," Luca grinned, "but a buddy of mine sent me a text after the game this morning. He told me that Timothy and Antonio found another team to play on, or their dads did. So guess which one?"

"Get outta here!" Paulo said.

The boys began talking all at once.

"Hold on," Kenneth said dramatically. "Do you have any idea what this means?" They stared at him. "We either beat the Storm or we have to kill ourselves."

"No point in living if we lose to Timothy and Antonio," Luca said.

"Then we'd better practise," Paulo said. He stole the ball from Kenneth and carried it to the middle of the field, Kenneth and Luca in hot pursuit. It didn't take long for a game of take-away to start up. Cody didn't play. He'd told them he was tired, and figured it would be strange for him to suddenly get the energy. After a few minutes, Kenneth flopped on the ground next to Cody.

"I looked for you after the game," Kenneth said quietly, "but you'd already gone. But Paulo said he had your phone number and email, so I didn't sweat it. We figured it might be more fun to meet here than hang at home all day."

His dad had been on the phone for at least an hour. Paulo probably tried to call, and then sent the email. "No big deal," Cody said. "I did a ton of stretching on my leg and stuff and had lunch. Sorry I was late."

Kenneth laughed. "You weren't late. We were early."

"You two gonna help out?" Luca said to them. "This guy won't let me play."

Paulo was bouncing the ball on his right foot. He knocked it up to his hip, slid his right foot behind his left leg and kicked the ball over Luca's head with his right instep. Luca jumped, but it was too high. Paulo zipped past him and within seconds was bouncing the ball on his right foot again.

Luca threw his hands up in the air. "I give up. You can keep it. I don't even like soccer, anyway."

Paulo kicked the ball to Cody and sat beside him. "Everyone's going to have to play haid the whole game or we're done for — and no subs," Paulo said, shaking his head.

"That does suck," Kenneth said, "although I'm happy to have a heart attack rather than have Timothy or John on the team."

"You're forgetting about our good buds, Antonio and Tyler," Luca said.

They let rip with a loud *hip-hip-hurrah.*

"It's nice of these losers to cheer us before we kick their butts," Cody heard someone say in a loud voice.

He turned to see Trane and Stick about ten metres away. "Trane, get a load of Baldy," Stick said. "What's up with that? His freakin' head glows."

Cody instinctively touched his head. He'd forgotten his skullcap. What an idiot.

"Private party, mates — maybe next year," Kenneth said, in a fake English accent.

Trane's eyes narrowed. "We don't wanna join your loser party," he snickered, and then pointed at Paulo. "If it ain't our old soccer buddy. You got my ball, I think."

"You're confused," Paulo said. "It was mine."

Trane took a few steps forward.

"You know this guy?" Kenneth asked Paulo.

"I do," Paulo said. "He's a king-sized jerk. He tried to steal my dad's soccer ball. That's how me and Cody met. Cody got it back for me."

Cody felt Trane's eyes swing over to him.

"I shoulda known you took the ball," Trane said. "You snagged it when me and Stick were playin' one-on-one. Don't ya know stealing is wrong?" He took another step forward.

Paulo got up. Luca and Kenneth did also. Cody scrambled to his feet, his ball under his left arm. Trane's fists were clenched. "I think I want that ball, little boys. Me and Stick wanna kick it around. We love soccer. Don't we?"

"I don't play soccer," Stick said.

"I said we like to play and we want that ball," Trane snarled.

"Yeah. Gotcha. I love soccer. It's my favourite thing to do in the whole world," Stick said.

"But we can't play if we don't have a ball," Trane said.

"That's tough for you," Paulo said. "You ain't gettin' this one."

Trane took another step forward. "And what makes you think that?"

"Come and get it," Paulo said. He thrust his chin forward.

Cody gripped the ball tightly. His heart was pounding, and he wanted to run away as fast as he could. These guys were big. But there was no way he was leaving. His teammates had invited him to the park, and he'd stand by them.

"Give me the ball or you'll feel it, believe me," Trane said. He punched his left hand with his fist.

"I think we'll keep it," Paulo said.

"Thanks for asking," Kenneth said.

"Maybe we can all play together another time," Luca said.

Cody was too scared to speak. For a terrifying few seconds Trane stared at each of them. His eyes were blazing and Cody thought he was going to attack them any moment. Then just like that Trane shrugged and elbowed Stick.

"You're right, bro. Soccer is the lamest game around. And these losers ain't worth our time. Let's go."

He turned his back on them and walked to the road.

Stick followed. Before he disappeared through the trees Stick looked back at them. No one said a word until they were gone.

"I'm really going to miss them," Kenneth said, "especially that Trane fellow."

"Stick will talk your ear off if you give him the chance," Luca added, and he, Kenneth, and Paulo burst out laughing. Cody was still too scared to laugh.

"I had them pegged as bullies, and a bully always backs down," Paulo said.

"No way I was gonna let them take Cody's ball," Kenneth declared.

"The Lions don't roll like that," Luca said.

"We roll to the championship," Kenneth said.

"Cody scores a few more goals, and we'll be holding that championship trophy no problem," Luca said.

"How awesome would it be to stuff a trophy in Timothy's face when we win?" Kenneth said.

"Why do you always forget John?" Luca said.

"Or Antonio and Tyler?" Paulo said.

"Or the Dragons?" Luca said.

"Or Anthony?" Paulo said.

Kenneth's face darkened. "Don't know what got into that guy. We were best friends in primary school. He totally changed, especially this year, hanging around with this totally bogus crew who think they own the school and are the coolest guys in the world."

"He can watch us win, too," Paulo said.

Cody kept a tight grip on his ball, as if he were keeping it safe for them all, as if for maybe the first time in a long time, maybe forever, he felt that he was really among friends. Already they'd been through a lot: the Super Subs, the Dragons, Timothy and John, the vote, the tournament, and now this. . . .

What next?

The referee's shrill whistle stopped the play.

"Hand ball! Hand ball!" Paulo repeated excitedly.

The game had barely started. The ref pointed to the spot. Antonio jumped up in the air and stomped on the ground.

"You've got to be kidding," Timothy screamed. "It was an accidental touch. He didn't move his hand or anything. Don't you know the rules?"

"I couldn't get my hand out of the way," Antonio said. "Brutal call. You wanna give the game to them?"

The ref reached into his pocket and pulled out a yellow card. He held it up toward Timothy, and then Antonio.

"Easy does it, Timmer," Ian yelled from the sidelines. "We need you in this. You'll get it back. Don't sweat it."

Timothy rolled his eyes and slapped his hands on his

thighs. Antonio glared at the ref, but he kept quiet also.

Funny thing was, Cody actually agreed with them. He'd booted the ball from just inside the box, and Antonio had been only a couple metres away. It looked like an accidental touch to him. Luca came running over.

"Coach wants Paulo to take the kick," he said.

A cocky grin spread across the Brazilian striker's face.

"No problem, Paulo. This is all yours," Kenneth said. He and Paulo bumped fists gently.

The crowd grew silent. The goalie took his spot on the line. Trevor had given them the lowdown on this team before the game. As Kenneth had said, the Storm liked to play tough defence and wait for the chance to counter-attack. An early goal would be huge because it would force the Storm to come out of their defensive shell.

Cody held his breath. Paulo took four quick steps forward and reared back with his right foot. The goalie dove to his left. Paulo chipped the ball softly toward the middle of the net. It wouldn't have broken an egg. But the goalie had committed too early, and the ball kissed the strings at the back of the net. It was a goal.

Only Paulo would have the guts to try something like that. Cody threw a fist in the air and joined his teammates as they crowded around the goal scorer.

"Awesome start, Lions," William said.

"They'll come back hard, though," Luca said.

"We got lucky," Kenneth said. "This is still gonna be a battle."

"Garbage goal," Timothy said to them. "Enjoy the lead for about two minutes until I totally smoke your back line."

"Scores on a penalty shot. Big deal," Antonio said.

"And thanks for that, by the way," Kenneth shot back. He pulled on Paulo's and Luca's shirts and they followed him up the pitch.

"You got something to say for once, Egg-Head?" Timothy said.

"I got nothing to say to you," Cody said without thinking. He left Timothy and Antonio standing there and he jogged back for the kickoff.

Paulo was waiting for him. "That was pure beauty," Cody said to him.

"You put this game away with the next one," Paulo said to him.

"Two-nothing sounds good to me," Cody replied. He pulled up on the Tensor bandage he'd wrapped around his right thigh.

Timothy sent the ball back to the right midfielder, who in turn rolled it to his back line. Paulo and Cody pushed forward to pressure. The right back calmly swung it wide to his left winger, spun, cut inside, and slid a hard pass to the left midfielder. From there it went to Timothy, and then wide right.

Cody and Paulo held their positions. Trevor had warned them about wasting energy running all over the place. Cody watched as the Storm did a nice job working it down the right side. About twenty metres from the penalty area, a winger attempted to penetrate inside, but he didn't reckon on Luca's quickness. Luca cut him off, and William came across to strip the ball away; without a moment's hesitation he fired it up to Kenneth, who promptly set off toward the Storm's end. Jordan had space on the right side, and Kenneth lofted a pass over a midfielder's head for him to run onto. Jordan took it cleanly and carried on at pace.

Paulo moved over to support. On a whim, Cody opted to go wide left. Jordan had a wicked right-footed cross, and if he could get even with a defender he'd have a chance for a header. Jordan put it square to Paulo, but instead of carrying it himself, Paulo took a step inside and rolled the ball between the two left defenders. Jordan was on it like a cat. The second he saw Jordan would get to it Cody poured it on.

The cross came, and the goalie underestimated Jordan's pinpoint accuracy and Cody's speed. The ball arced way over the goalie's outstretched fingers. Cody almost laughed as he headed the ball into the open net. Two goals, just like that. Let Timothy and Antonio open their big mouths now. This game was as good as won.

★★★

David threw his body across the goal line. Almost horizontal, he punched the ball with his fists, deflecting it ever so slightly. It nicked the outside of the post for a corner. Timothy kicked at the ground and punched a fist in the air. He'd just missed tying it up. The nimble goalie leapt to his feet.

"Come on, Lions. Clear the ball," David urged.

Trevor waved his arms frantically. "Cody, Paulo, everyone back for this corner."

Cody ran to the box, although run was maybe an exaggeration. He was so tired he could barely move. His leg ached and his breathing was so laboured his chest hurt. After the second goal, the Storm had taken control of the game, and their attack had been relentless. Twenty minutes into the second half Timothy had scored after a mad scramble in the box, and so now the Lions clung to a precarious one-goal lead.

"Mark someone," Luca said.

Luca had been a one-man wall at times, blocking shots and heading the ball out of harm's way. Nearby, Kenneth shoved against Timothy for position. Antonio ran up and stationed himself right beside David.

"C'mon, ref. Give me a break. This guy's all over me," Timothy yelled.

"I just wanna be your friend," Kenneth said.

"You're an idiot." Timothy pushed him away.

"I know you don't mean that." Kenneth pushed back.

"Cut it out," the ref barked at them, "or you'll be sent off."

Timothy growled under his breath, but he backed away and let Kenneth take the inside position closest to the net.

"I need a body on the near post! Wake up, guys!" David pleaded, and Jacob raced over. "Cody, you cover Antonio," he ordered.

The goalie was in charge of defence on set pieces. Cody reluctantly slipped in next to him. The Storm winger set the ball down. An elbow dug into Cody's arm.

"Touch me and you die," Antonio said under his breath

Cody felt a momentary flash of fear — and then a surge of anger.

172

"You ain't got nothing, Egg-Head," Antonio said. "This is a game for big boys."

"Let's go, Storm! Let's go!"

The crowd was making tons of noise, and the Storm parents had kept up a constant cheer practically from the moment they'd gotten their goal. Ian's and Antonio's dads hadn't stopped yelling at the ref the entire game. The whistle blew and the cheering got louder. The kick came into the box, curving high. Antonio tried to shove Cody aside; Cody kept his feet and leapt as high as he could. Antonio went up as well, but it was Cody who got his head on the ball and directed it out of bounds for another corner.

"Atta boy, Cody," Kenneth chimed.

But Cody wasn't listening. He was on the pitch clutching his leg. Antonio had sucker-punched him right on the Tensor bandage. The pain was intense but already fading, so he knew he'd be okay. Then he saw his mom, panic-stricken, coming onto the pitch. He'd never live this down.

Cody rolled onto his side and looked over, meeting his mom's eyes. She stopped a few metres inside the sideline. He blinked a few times to stop the tears, not from the pain but from the humiliation of what was to come. His mom put her hands to her mouth, and then slowly let them drop to her sides. She closed her eyes and turned back.

Cody took a moment to mentally thank her, and then forced himself to his knees and on to his feet. The last thing the Lions needed was to be a man short.

"Are you okay, number seventeen?" the referee asked.

Cody nodded emphatically. The ref had called a fair game, and Cody was sure he'd have red-carded Antonio if he'd seen the punch. He'd have to be on his guard, though. Antonio probably had more ugly tricks up his sleeve.

"Total delay of game, ref," Timothy complained. "He has to go off."

The referee blew his whistle, swinging his arm windmill fashion to signal the start of play. Timothy looked up to the sky and groaned. "This ref is an idiot," he said aloud.

"Let's actually mark a man this time, Lions," David yelled, and he clapped his hands a few times.

"You afraid to head the ball?" Cody said to Antonio. "Don't you want to tie the game up?"

"You should've gone off when you had the chance, Egg-Head," Antonio said. "Next time I'm breaking your leg."

The winger lofted the ball into the box. Antonio gathered himself for the header. Cody gave Antonio a sharp elbow to the ribs before his feet left the ground, and then went up for the header himself, knocking the ball forward. A midfielder kicked it back in.

The next second he was knocked off his feet. Something had hit him on the side of his head. Cody was livid. He'd had enough of Antonio to last a lifetime. Then he felt someone pull him up.

"I hit you by accident," David said. "Sorry. Ball is to the right."

So it hadn't been Antonio. Cody looked around to find the ball. Unfortunately, it found him — right in the forehead. Stunned, he lurched back, struggling to remain standing. The ball was a metre away and he threw out his left foot. He didn't get much on it and the ball bounced forward. Timothy cut over and connected with his left foot. The ball rocketed toward the goal, this time right into Paulo's stomach.

Paulo let out a gasp and dropped to one knee. The ball bounced to Austin and the defender spun and kicked it wildly. He sliced it and the ball went up and toward the net. David jumped and punched his fist at the ball.

The line judge held up his flag. The ball had nicked the crossbar and bounced into touch.

Cody held the bottom of his shorts with one hand and rubbed his forehead with the other.

"You okay, Paulo?" he asked.

Paulo shrugged as if nothing had happened. He and a Storm attacker were already pushing each other for position, about six metres from the line. Kenneth and Timothy pushed against each other, too. Antonio didn't say a word as Cody braced himself for the third corner in a row. This time it was a line drive to a Storm winger down low, his back to the goal. He cleverly flicked it on into the middle of the box. Kenneth and Cody, along with Timothy and Antonio, went up for it.

The next thing Cody knew, he was sitting on the ground facing Kenneth.

"Maybe one of us should call it next time," Kenneth said ruefully. He rubbed the side of his head.

Cody rubbed the top of his. He was going to have one nasty bump.

"Another stupid corner," Timothy said. "Let's get this already, Storm."

"You or me headed it out," Kenneth said, getting slowly

to his feet. "And yeah, it's another corner."

This time they took their spots automatically. The ball came in fairly high and it sailed over Cody's head. He turned to follow as William and a Storm player fought for position. The sturdy defender prevailed and headed it to the sidelines. Unfortunately, a winger ran it down and, quick as a flash, spun and sent a dangerous cross right back.

This time Luca was there, diving at the ball to head it outside the box. Cody hurried after it. The Lions had to get control of the ball, or at least get it outside their zone to relieve the pressure. The Storm had left one player back and he got to it first, calmly passing it wide right. The exhausted Lions had barely moved forward and so the pass was onside.

The cross came hard and fast, and again Luca knocked it away. The ball bounced to the right and Cody shifted across.

Thud!

The ball rocketed off Cody's shoulder and spun crazily into the middle of the box. It was pandemonium now. The Lions kicked and headed the ball with fury and threw themselves around the pitch in a feverish attempt to keep the Storm from tying the game.

A total frenzy.

First Ryan, and then Austin blocked point-blank shots from Timothy; then, David absolutely robbed the Storm when he deflected a shot destined for the top corner to the right of the post with a miraculous fingertip save.

"Not another corner," Kenneth complained.

"Better than a goal," Luca said, clapping his buddy on the back.

The ball came in about two and a half metres high, but close to the goal. David shot out and reached over Cody and Antonio, crashing to the pitch. Cody felt like giving the acrobatic goaltender a hug, for clutched in his hands, pressed against his chest, was the ball. The Lions finally had possession. David could at the very least thump the ball downfield and relieve the pressure, if only for a minute.

But he never had to.

The referee blew his whistle three times, and the Lions' parents began to cheer like mad.

"Brutal game," Timothy roared. "Can't believe that penalty shot. Most bogus call ever." He slapped his hands together and marched to the sidelines.

"Next time, Egg-Head," Antonio muttered. "Next time." He followed Timothy.

Cody lowered himself to one knee. They'd actually won. It didn't seem possible. Kenneth, Luca, and Paulo came over and knelt next to him. All of them were too tired to say a word. David joined next, then the rest of the back line, and finally Jordan, Brandon, and Austin.

Kenneth broke the silence. "That was gut-check time, guys. That was a total team win. We're in the finals — and no one thought we had a chance."

Suddenly, Cody didn't feel quite so tired or sore. Come to think of it, he felt great! Surrounded by his teammates, his energy flooded back.

So what that they had no substitutes.

So what that his leg hurt.

So what that he got punched in the leg, a ball in the forehead, and had banged heads with Kenneth.

The Lions were in the finals.
They'd beaten Timothy and Antonio.
It was trophy time!

Cody ran his fingers gently above his eyebrow. The skin was all red and looked nasty where the ball had hit him. He wasn't worried about that, however. Overnight, in the spot where Antonio had punched him, his leg had stiffened up tight as a board — literally. He couldn't bend it.

Just great. He had to play in four hours and he looked like a zombie and couldn't walk.

Cody hobbled to the bathroom and splashed some cold water on his face. Bad move! It stung so bad he had to stuff a towel into his mouth to stifle a scream. He heaved a sigh and straight-legged it down the stairs and over to the kitchen.

"So maybe we can swing by and pick up the new carpet before the game," he heard his mom say. "It'll fit in the trunk, and then we can go out for lunch after."

"That'll be good," his dad mumbled.

"You're coming, right?" his mom asked sharply.

Cody crept closer. He saw his dad peer over his newspaper. "Yes, I'm coming to watch Cody play in the finals against the best team in the league, the undefeated and dreaded United."

She clapped her hands together and laughed, which made Cody laugh, too. There hadn't been much laughing in their house for a long time, but during the tournament his mom and dad had been kinda . . . goofy together, like they used to be before he got sick.

His mom turned around. "Hey, there. You want a cheese omelette with an English muffin for breakfast? We want to leave a bit early to run an errand before the big game, so you need to eat now."

Cody tried to hide it, but his mom's face fell as soon as he walked into the kitchen.

"My goodness, Cody. Are you kidding me?"

He limped to the table and dropped onto a chair. Suddenly, he had to fight back tears. "I woke up and I could barely bend my leg. I took a hot bath and tried stretching, but it made no difference. That idiot punched me on the outside of my leg and gave me another charley horse. I can't play and we'll never win against United with ten players. What am I gonna do?"

His dad cleared his throat. "It's not your fault you got hurt. If you can't play, then that's the way it is. Are you allowed to play with ten?"

Cody's chin dropped. His teammates would hate him.

His mom was probing his leg gently.

"What are you doing?" he asked.

"Show me where it hurts," she instructed.

Cody pointed half-heartedly to the side of his right thigh.

"It doesn't hurt at . . . the back?"

There it was. She'd never let him play. "No. It's on the side, I said."

His mom scrunched her mouth to one side. "Good. Then there's nothing to worry about."

His dad lowered his newspaper.

"You need to run," she said. "Sitting is the worst thing. Why don't we start with a brisk walk around the block and go from there?"

Cody shrugged. "No point. It's like a board. I can't move, let alone run. It's totally messed."

"How about you try, and we'll see if it helps," she said.

"It won't."

"We could try."

"It's a waste of time."

"Listen to me, Cody," his mom said. "You're the one who wanted to play more than life itself. You're the one who begged and pleaded, and then begged some more. You have a charley horse. Okay. You're going to quit that easily? Soccer's a tough sport, and you better get used to injuries. I had more than my share, believe me. Now get up and let's go for that walk."

Cody sat back in his chair.

She looked into his eyes. "Would you do it for your mom and dad?"

He didn't answer.

She laughed and raised her eyebrows. "How about for the Lions Football Club?"

He rolled his neck and stood up. "I guess a little walk wouldn't kill me."

His dad folded his newspaper and put in on the table. "I guess a walk wouldn't kill me either. I think I'll join you. It's not every day we get a chance for a family stroll, and I could use the exercise, too." He patted his stomach and grinned.

His mom patted his dad's arm. "Follow me, boys, and keep up."

Minutes later the three of them were walking along the sidewalk. Cody felt ridiculous, like a little kid. For the first time since they'd moved to this neighbourhood he was glad he didn't know anyone. At first the leg really hurt, even though they went slowly, but after a couple of blocks he was able to walk at a fairly normal pace.

"Your leg seems to be better, no?" his mom asked.

"Feels better, for sure. I guess it was a good idea."

"What do you mean *was*? Besides, it's not over. Now we jog, really slow."

"Awesome. There's nothing I love more than a good run," his dad said.

Cody gave him a look. He never exercised. His mom was always bugging him about his fitness. But there were his dad and mom running ahead, and while he felt dumb jogging with his parents, he figured he had no choice but to keep up. It took awhile, but they finally made it around the block and back to the house. He stopped on the driveway, rubbing his leg. It still hurt like anything.

His mom was running backwards along the sidewalk. "Who said we were done, lazy boy? Let's pick up the pace."

"Forget it, mom. It's not going to work."

She slowed, still going backwards "So I'll just have to tell your teammates that your old mom ran you into the ground."

"Nice try. My leg is useless."

"Poor baby. Codesy-Wodesy is all tired."

This was irritating. As if she could keep up if he were a hundred per cent.

"Let's go around one more time," his dad suggested. He was sweating and breathing heavily.

"You sure about that?" Cody said.

"I'll carry Cody if it gets too hard for him," his mom added.

His parents were acting totally weird. "Whatever," Cody said. He knew they'd fall apart soon. They couldn't keep up. For the first block they did, though, which was totally annoying; and by the halfway mark they were still with him. Cody picked up the pace. This was stupid. He wasn't losing a race to his mom and dad.

"Is this slow enough for you?" his mom said to Cody. She was breathing pretty hard.

They turned the corner together. The house came into view, about two hundred metres away. His mom sprinted past him — and then his dad! His chunky dad, the guy whose belly jiggled when he ran, the guy who couldn't run five metres without being exhausted, *that* guy was beating him!

Cody began to all-out sprint. They'd tease him about

this forever. The parked cars made it impossible for him to pass on the street. He kept trying to get by on the sidewalk, but between his mom's weaving and his dad's elbows there wasn't any room. With twenty metres to go, still stuck behind them, Cody ran onto their next-door neighbour's lawn and managed to pull even. He glanced over. His dad was gasping for breath and his face was beet-red and covered in sweat. His mom was grunting loudly, pumping her arms high up in the air.

"Have fun with the hedge," his dad said.

A short hedge divided the properties. "Unfair," Cody said.

"Life's not fair," his dad said.

"Fine," he said. He didn't care. He was going to win or die trying. He let out a yell and threw his right leg up, hurdler style. It skimmed the top of the hedge, and he was just able to drag his left leg over. It caught momentarily on a branch and he almost fell, but at the last second he regained his balance. But he had no time to worry about the close call. There were a few metres to go, and go he did. He inched past his mom just before they reached the driveway. He threw his arms up on the air. His mom groaned and she staggered to a stop, bending over with her hands on her knees, breathing heavily. His dad thundered in after them and threw himself down on their front lawn.

"I have two things to say," his dad said between gasps. "I've run enough for today, and Cody's leg is fine."

Cody reached down. He'd totally forgotten about it. His mom and dad were laughing, and he had to join in.

"Let's put a heating pad on it," his mom said, "and then

you can do some stretching." She had to take a few more breaths before continuing. "We'll wrap it with a Tensor bandage, and you should be okay. What do you say?"

"I'll do without the Tensor; it's too much of a target. But the rest sounds good," Cody said

He forced himself to stay calm in front of his parents. His mom had been right. All he needed to do was run. The leg still hurt, but the pain was totally manageable. He and his mom went to the front door.

"Are you coming, dear?" his mom called out.

"I think I'll lie down for a few more minutes," his dad said. "I never noticed how soft our grass is."

"Take your time," his mom said. "We'll scrape you off the lawn before we go."

"Thanks for caring."

His mom put her arm around Cody's shoulders, and they went inside to find the heating pad.

"You got these losers, United. Easy win. Total joke team. Time to run up the score." Timothy clapped for the United players as they came off the pitch after the first half. Ian and Antonio were next to him, clapping just as hard.

"Don't worry about that," Trevor said. "Let me have your attention here."

Cody hadn't really noticed them. Funny how terrified he used to be of those guys. Things had sure changed in a hurry. Kenneth passed a water bottle to Cody, who took a couple of swigs before giving it to Luca.

Trevor tapped the whiteboard where he'd just finished sketching a formation. "Not the best first half, but not the worst," he began slowly. "We're down two-nil, but that's the lowest number of goals United has scored in the first half this whole tournament."

"That's not the record we want, coach," Paulo said. "We wanna win."

"I'm with you on that," Trevor concurred. He pointed to Leandro. "My new assistant coach, manager, and trainer, who happened to play professional soccer for two of the best teams in Brazil and who also happens to be a doctor, has an idea, and I think it's a good one."

The players huddled closer.

"We've been playing a 4-1-4-1, which I thought made sense because it's defensive enough against United's explosive offence but still allowed us some chance to attack."

Cody had seen the logic of it, and the formation slowed United down. But the Lions had struggled to get any shots. He wondered what these two ex-pros had up their sleeves.

Trevor jabbed his pen on the whiteboard. "We're going to switch things up and go with the 3-4-1-2. Paulo, instead of being a holding midfielder, I want you to roam between the strikers and the midfielders. You're going to have to work hard because you need to help cover the middle with William. Defenders should look to get him the ball, and Paulo, it's up to you to distribute to the open man. Leandro, talk to them about the wingers."

Leandro knelt beside the whiteboard. His eyes were shining brightly. "This formation doesn't work unless you have skilled wingers who can push up the sidelines to pressure the defence, but who also have the stamina and the heart to get back to defend." He nodded at Kenneth and Luca. "We think you two are those players. You have to look for chances to attack, and then send strong crosses into the penalty area, especially to Cody."

Cody   Jordan

Paulo

Kenneth   Ryan   Brandon   Luca

Austin   William   Jacob

David

"Listen up, Lions," Trevor said. "It's getting hot, and I know you're tired after playing three games with only eleven players. But if you really want to win this thing, you have to play harder than United. You have to want to win more. A normal effort won't cut it, an above-average effort won't either; you need the effort of your lives. Two goals is nothing. We can do this. I believe in this team. Think how much you've overcome already."

"And think how cool it'll be when we win this tournament," Kenneth shouted.

"This is our game," Paulo sounded.

He and Kenneth bumped fists.

"Time to show United not to mess with Lions," Luca said.

Cody stood up. "You cross those balls in," he said solemnly, "and I'll score those goals."

Everyone was quiet for a moment, and then they exploded in cheers and high-fives, returning to the pitch chanting "*Li-ons . . . Li-ons . . . Li-ons.*"

Cody was having trouble believing what he'd just said.

He had promised to score two goals in one half against United!

Paulo interrupted his thoughts. "Don't worry about coming back to play defence," Paulo said. "You get in a spot to score, and I'll get the ball to you."

Kenneth came over. "United hasn't been in a close game all season. They'll think they've got this game wrapped up. We score first, and they'll panic."

His friends broke away to take their positions. Cody stood at the circle waiting for the kick off. United was lined up in a 4-4-2, a strongly defensive formation and a tough nut to crack. Marco, the star defender who had given them such a tough time in the first league game, was organizing his teammates.

"Our ball, United," Marco said. "We want it on the deck. Simple game of keep-away, and look for a chance to counter-attack."

Obviously, Marco didn't care if the Lions heard: control the ball, keep eight players back, and attack if the chance presented itself. It made sense, and they had the talent to do it. Cody felt his leg. It throbbed a bit, but a little pain wouldn't stop him. He'd made a promise to his teammates.

He'd promised two goals.

★★★

As the second half unfolded, United's defence proved to be more than a tough nut; it was more like a steel curtain. With Marco storming across the back line and his team- mates committed to team defence, Cody wondered if he'd made an empty promise. There couldn't be more than fifteen minutes left, and he hadn't taken a single good shot. On the plus side, the score remained 2–0, and no one had been that close to United this season. It was frustrating, all the same; like Paulo said, they wanted to win, not lose, not even to the best team.

David set the ball down at the six-yard marker and booted it to the far right to Jordan. A United midfielder got position and headed the ball back to the Lions' half. Luca ran down the errant ball and passed it square inside to Jacob, who fed it over to William. William pressed forward, and then backed it up and sent it the other way to Austin. Cody drifted across the pitch following the ball, fighting a growing sense of hopelessness. The two United lines were following the ball as well, a double wall the Lions couldn't penetrate. The idea of a wall triggered a memory of an old kid's song, for some bizarre reason: "Going on a lion hunt; Gonna catch a big one." In the song, you got to an obstacle, like a wall, and you either went around, under, through, or over. It occurred to Cody that the Lions had tried going around and through again and again. Under was definitely not an option. Maybe it was time for the over?

Paulo was ten metres away. Cody ran to him.

"I got an idea," Cody said to him, with growing excitement. "If you get the ball, send a long, high pass down the sidelines and I'll try to run onto it. It's the only way to beat this defence."

Paulo's eyes sparkled and he raced off, calling for the ball. Cody knew he could count on Paulo to do his part. He had to do his, and he forced his tired body to the right side. Luca had the ball and he was pressing forward slowly, probing in vain for a weakness in United's formation.

Luca answered Paulo's call and passed it. Cody drifted up the pitch as far as he could without being offside, and then hunched over and grabbed the bottom of his shorts, pretending to be too exhausted to be of any concern to the United defenders. Paulo swerved to the right, looking very casual as he surveyed the pitch. He faked a pass to Jordan, faked another wide left to Kenneth, and then carried it further to the right himself. To the players and the crowd it looked as if Paulo didn't know what to do. Only Cody could see what his crafty teammate was up to, because ever so slowly, metre by metre, he was pushing the ball forward, until he was about ten metres behind the centre line.

Suddenly, Paulo darted upfield and cut hard to the sidelines. When he was about four metres from the line he launched a massive strike. Cody anticipated the pass and he took off the moment the ball left Paulo's foot. The ball whistled over the left back's head. Cody knew he was onside and he didn't have to slow down. He got control of the bouncing ball and wheeled toward the United goal, the rest of the defenders, led by Marco, hustling to cut him off.

United's goaltender came out about ten metres, expecting a shot, and Cody knew he had to let it go soon or Marco would catch him. He shuffled the ball onto his left foot to shoot. Marco took a huge stride and leapt in front of Cody.

Cody groaned as he trapped the ball and turned his

back to the net, furious with himself. He should've shot faster. He'd promised to score, and when all he had to do was shoot with his right leg, he'd gotten scared. He cut toward the middle of the field, hoping to gain time for support to reach him.

"Shoot!" he heard Kenneth scream from midfield.

Cody looked up. He couldn't believe it. His sudden move had taken the United defenders by surprise. No one had expected him to stop short on a breakaway and spin away; even Marco had overrun him, and now Cody had another clear shot on goal. Even better, he could shoot with his left foot. He took a short step, and then powered it with every ounce of strength he had. He hadn't struck a ball like that in ages, not since before he got sick.

Marco jumped up to head the ball away — and missed. The goalie leapt to his left, his arm extended overhead. The ball hit his hand.

"Goal! Goal! Goal!" Kenneth screamed in Cody's ear, his arms wrapped around his neck.

The force of the shot had been too much for the goalie and the ball had blasted past him and into the net. Paulo arrived next.

"You had me worried for a sec. Never seen a guy let defenders catch him on a breakaway. I guess you wanted to make the highlight reel," Paulo said. He gave Cody a hug.

The rest of the Lions charged downfield to congratulate him.

"We got more work to do," Kenneth said to them. "Let's line up and win this game already. I want that trophy." He led them back to centre. Cody followed behind, his thoughts focused on his promise. That was the first one. He needed one more.

The next ten minutes of the game were a complete opposite to what had happened up to that point. Stoked by Cody's goal, the Lions played better than they had all season, keeping possession practically the entire time, while United defended desperately. Time was running short, however, and Cody felt himself feeling more and more desperate. Ryan held the ball over his head for a throw-in about twenty-five metres from the United goal line. Cody cut sharply in between two defenders, which attracted their attention, and that allowed Paulo to slip away from the defender marking him. Ryan delivered the ball, and Paulo drilled a pass to Brandon, hovering in the middle of the pitch. Kenneth made himself available and received a pass.

Cody was standing even with the United back line, but they began to step up to force Cody to retreat to stay onside. Harried by the ever-present Marco, Kenneth had to give up ground. Paulo was free in the middle, and Kenneth rolled it over. This little cat-and-mouse game continued, with the Lions pushing to the penalty area only to be forced to send the ball to the flank or back to a midfielder. Cody raced from sideline to sideline, hoping to slip through a crack in the United armour. A couple of times he thought he was free, but the ball carrier, whether it was Paulo, Kenneth, Brandon, or Jordan, feared giving up possession and instead passed it elsewhere.

"Patience, lads," Trevor repeated several times as this was going on. "Keep the ball. Keep the ball. We need possession."

"Nice and slow, and use the whole pitch," Leandro added.

It was hard not to panic, but Cody forced himself to calm down and work the ball around and the rest of his teammates did the same. Paulo took a pass from Jacob on the right side some ten metres from the sidelines, and then whirled and pressed forward toward the United goal. Two defenders shifted over to bar his path. Cody stayed wide left. Paulo would have to pull it back again, anyway, and he didn't see the point in running over. Paulo had other ideas, however; he certainly didn't lack for confidence, and who else on the team would even think to flick the ball with his right foot to his own head, and then knock it past two very surprised United players?

Cody charged into the box like a wild bull. Two defenders shifted over to mark him. Paulo took another step and delivered the cross. Sandwiched between defenders, Cody strained his neck to reach the ball. Maybe because he swung his head a little harder, or maybe because he wanted it more, but for whatever reason Cody got his head on it first and he struck the ball cleanly. The second it left his head, he knew. He'd made good on his promise. Like a rocket, the ball streaked past the goaltender's right hand — and bounced right off the crossbar.

Cody stared as if aliens had landed on earth. That wasn't fair. That wasn't right. No time left, probably their last chance, and he hits the crossbar!

A United defender took the ball off his chest and swung his right foot to clear it. Kenneth flashed past Cody and stretched out his leg. The ball deflected off Kenneth's foot and bounced high in the air. For a second time Cody leapt at the ball; only this time, the goalie beat him to it and punched it away. Paulo was closest to the ball and he settled under it. To Cody it looked like Paulo had misjudged it, however. He was about to tell him to back up when he checked himself.

"Bicycle kick," Cody said in disbelief.

His back practically parallel to the ground and his feet spinning as if pedalling a bike, Paulo's right foot connected with the ball, sending a bullet blasting in on goal. The goalie didn't move. No one did. They all watched the ball sail past the helpless keeper and into the net.

Cody threw his hands in the air. Kenneth leapt up, a fist held aloft. Marco grabbed his head with both hands.

"That's the most outrageous goal I've ever seen," Kenneth said. He wrapped an arm around Paulo's shoulders.

"The most outrageous goal of all time," Luca said.

"Awesome, Lions. Awesome," William said.

The referee's whistle blasted, and all the players, Lions and United alike, turned to look at him. Their faces must have asked the question.

"It's overtime, boys," the ref said with a slight smile. "And if that doesn't settle it, we go to a shootout."

The Lions ran off the pitch as if the game hadn't even started. Trevor and Leandro had more than a little trouble calming them down; even the parents got into it, and Trevor had to shush them a few times after his players had quieted. Cody snuck a glance at his mom and dad. She had led the way clapping the Lions off the pitch, which didn't surprise him much. What he couldn't get over was his dad. He'd totally lost it, cheering away and hugging other parents.

"I've seen and played in thousands of games and that was one of the most exciting finishes of all time," Trevor enthused.

"Showed a great deal of character," Leandro said. "Well done, Lions."

"But if you want to win the overtime you have to forget

what just happened," Trevor said. "The time to celebrate Paulo's goal is over. You had your chance to enjoy. Now it's in the past — the far past. So listen up. There's lots of soccer left. We have two twenty-minute periods, and then a shoot out if need be. We'll stick with the same formation, but the wingers must be more careful on defence. United won't stay in a defensive shell. I bet you they'll come out hard, so we need to keep it conservative for the first couple of minutes. When we get control of the ball, I want everyone to look for Paulo; and Paulo, I want you to place a few more long balls to Cody. That worked well on the first goal. If Cody gets possession, then we send Paulo, Jordan, Kenneth, and Brandon in support. Everyone else stays back . . . and hopefully, we'll punch it in."

"What about the shootout, coach?" Kenneth asked.

Trevor closed his eyes briefly, and laughed. "We'll figure something out. I'd rather win it in OT, so I don't have to suffer."

Kenneth jumped to his feet. "Not a problem. Easy-peasy. One goal it is. You boys ready?"

His teammates answered the challenge: "*Li-ons, Li-ons, Li-ons.*"

Kenneth held his hand out. "Let's have everyone in," he said, waiting for his teammates to add their hands into the circle. "This is our time, boys," Kenneth said. "I bet you Ian and Timothy and Antonio and John and the Dragons and that whole gang thought we'd lose in the round robin by big scores. They thought they'd have a good laugh at us. Looks to me like we might've surprised them. Looks to me like we finally have a team that plays like a team

Looks to me like we have a team that's gonna win this tournament."

A few boys murmured their approval.

"United think they're the best team in the league. They figure we just got lucky. They won't be giving us much respect. Wait for a mistake. Wait for it. When it comes, we pounce — and then we need to be unselfish and give the ball up to Paulo and Cody. They're the guys who will score."

Cody wished he hadn't said that, and then it got worse.

"Cody promised us two goals," Paulo said. "So I figure we got this game won."

"The Mailman always delivers," Kenneth said.

"You got this one, Cody," Luca said.

Cody knew his face was beet-red.

"Give me Lions on three," Kenneth roared. "One . . . two . . . three . . ."

"*Li-ons!*"

They threw their hands in the air, and then peeled off to take their positions.

"It's victory time," Luca yelled.

"Let's lay on the big hurt," William said, trotting off.

Cody walked to centre.

"Yo, Cody."

It was Paulo. He looked straight into Cody's eyes.

"You can do this," he said. "You just gotta believe that you can."

Before Cody could answer Paulo ran off to take his place in front of the midfielders. What a spot to be in. He felt a little sick to his stomach. And what was Paulo getting at? Believe what? Of course he wanted to score, but he didn't think United would just step aside and let him shoot on an open net.

He looked to the sidelines and saw his mom and dad standing among the other Lions parents. They were chanting *Go, Lions, Go*. It sure would be cool to score the winner. It would make his parents happy and they hadn't been happy for a long time.

★★★

Marco trapped the ball five metres outside his own box and spread it square to the left outside midfielder, who immediately pushed it up the sidelines. Cody watched from the middle of the pitch. He marvelled at his coach's insight. United had come out flying, as if they were angry at the Lions for tying the game. They'd nearly won it early on a corner kick, and up to this point, with a few minutes left in the first overtime period, the Lions hadn't had much possession.

The ball carrier pressed forward until Jordan and Brandon stepped up to force a pass. And what a pass! A beautiful chip found its way onto the foot of a United striker. Cody fought the urge to run back. Trevor had told him to look for the long ball from Paulo and so he needed to stay up front.

The striker cut across the field toward Austin, while his teammates poured in to support. Cody could tell the striker had no intention of passing and his heart sank. Austin had done his best this game, but he was the Lions' weakest player, no two ways about it. Sure enough, Austin held out his foot too tentatively, and the striker was past him in a flash. The crowd was going absolutely berserk.

David spread his arms wide, shifting his weight from foot to foot, waiting for the striker to make the first move. The striker had a ton of pace and way too much net to shoot at, however. All he had to do was fake one way and blast it the other. The game would be over, just like that.

As Cody predicted, the striker stutter-stepped and faked a shot, freezing David in his tracks. Here it comes, Cody said to himself.

But he was wrong.

Instead, the striker planted his right foot and sliced the ball with the outside of his left. It was a cheeky move, and it would've been a spectacular goal, only he hadn't counted on David's incredible flexibility and reflexes. The goaltender flung his right foot out, practically doing the splits, and his toe caught a piece of the ball. It still bounced toward the goal, but slowly enough to let Luca knock it out of harm's way. The ball came to Austin.

"Quick. Austin. Pass," Paulo yelled.

Austin passed it over and Paulo took off. Cody figured he'd carry it over midfield and look to set up the attack, but something about the way Paulo approached the ball convinced Cody otherwise. Paulo darted to the left and swung his foot. Here was the first long ball in OT.

Cody didn't even look; he just ran. The ball flew over his head and past the United back line. Cody took it without breaking stride and carried it in on goal. He felt the wind on his face, and in the background he could hear the sounds of the cheering spectators, muffled as if he were in a glass bubble. In fact, he felt as if he were playing soccer by himself in the park — nothing but him, the ball, and the goalie.

The goalie had edged out and moved to his right. That was weird. Why give him the other side of the net? Suddenly, Cody understood what Paulo had said to him. A striker doesn't worry about hurting himself. A striker does anything he can to score; he uses all his skills every time he touches the ball. This goalie didn't believe Cody would use his right foot. He'd seen Cody kicking all game with his left; he'd even seen him hold up on a breakaway to shoot with his left. Cody had been shying away from his right foot all season, and now it had become a habit.

A few steps inside the box the goalie came out to challenge. The sound of cleats grew louder behind Cody. He gritted his teeth, planted his left foot, and struck the ball solidly with his right. Time stood still. The crowd roared. He felt a pain shoot up the back of his right leg. The goalie dropped to his knees. Cody slowed down.

There it was.

Nestled in the back of the twine.

The ball.

A goal.

He'd kept his promise.

What felt like a hundred bodies knocked him to the ground and piled on, each one was screaming at the top of his lungs. Cody had no idea who was actually on top, and he didn't care. They were Lions — his teammates.

One by one they finally peeled themselves off, and

Cody could get to his feet. Kenneth, Luca, and Paulo continued to pound him on the back, pulling him toward the sidelines where their coaches and parents were clapping and cheering just as loudly as the players.

His teammates screamed and whooped and yelled the team name over and over, as if the victory had stolen their words. Of course, it was Kenneth who finally pulled together a sentence.

"*Give it up for the Lions!*"

In unison the players roared, and even a few parents joined in.

"I've changed my mind," Trevor bellowed over the noise. "This is definitely the most exciting game I've ever seen." The players took that as another excuse to let loose a massive roar. "I'd like to invite you all, parents and families included, to my house for a celebration. I've got the directions here, so grab a sheet from me before you go."

Parents crowded around Trevor.

"So are you going straight there, or what?" Kenneth asked Cody

Cody didn't think they'd go. His dad didn't like crowds and parties, and since he'd watched the game Cody bet he'd want to do some office work.

"I kinda doubt it," he said, thumbing behind him. "My parents probably have stuff to do."

Kenneth's mouth gaped open. "Our leading scorer has to be there. Hey, guys," he shouted.

"Don't worry about it," Cody whispered.

Kenneth ignored him. "Cody says he can't go to Trevor's."

A chorus of "Come on, Cody" and "No way" followed.

"I'll go ask my parents if we can take you," Kenneth asked. "I'm sure it'll be no problem. Wait here."

Kenneth sure had a way of complicating his life. This was becoming a big deal, and his dad would be mad at being forced to go. He spotted them talking to Leandro near the parking lot and he went over, figuring they'd get going before Kenneth could ask his parents.

Leandro's face lit up when he saw Cody. "I loved that goal," he said. "Took a great deal of courage to . . . make that shot."

Cody flushed. Made him wonder who else knew. "Thanks, Leandro. I got lucky, I guess."

"It's hard work that brings about that kind of luck. You've got a special player here, Cheryl," he said. "A pure goal-scorer, a real striker. They're hard to find."

"Cody loves to play," his mom said, "and your son is absolutely amazing. I've never seen a boy his age handle the ball so well. It's like he was born with a ball glued to his feet."

Leandro smiled. "In some ways he was. He started playing when he was eight months old, and I don't think he's ever stopped."

"Our boys make a good pair," she said. "It would have been fun for them to play together the rest of the season."

"Why aren't we playing together?" Cody asked sharply.

"I don't think you can get through the season with only eleven players," she said, "and I doubt you can recruit new players at this level now. This will have to be our championship." She sounded a bit sad.

Cody was devastated. It never occurred to him. Of course, she was right. He was being stupid. You can't play with eleven players. One injury and they'd be done for.

"I hope to see you at Trevor's house," Leandro said. "I just want to talk to Paulo for a second. Excuse me — and again, great game, Cody."

Cody fought back the tears. A minute ago he'd scored the golden goal, and now the Lions were done. No more soccer. No more friends.

23

"Where are we going?" Cody asked from the backseat.

"That's a good question," his dad replied. "What was the address again?"

"It's three-forty-three Pinewood Avenue," his mom said. "Are you sure we didn't miss the turn back there?"

"Is this the carpet place?" Cody asked. "Sure doesn't look like it." They were on a side street, for some reason.

"We don't have time for the carpet shop," his mom said. "What's that sign say up ahead, Sean?"

"Then why are we here?" Cody said.

His mom turned to face him. "Didn't you hear your coach invite the team over to his house?"

Cody had assumed they wouldn't go. "Sorry. Spaced out there a bit. No problem." At least now he could say good-bye to all the guys, he thought.

"Don't worry," his mom said. "We're almost in control. We'll find it soon." She looked hard at the map. "Turn right, Sean!"

The wheel's screeched as they turned the corner. His dad was grinning from ear to ear.

"How's that for a super spy turn, Cody?" he said.

"Not bad," he said. When Cody was a little boy he and his dad used to pretend to be spies. He really wished his dad would forget about that.

"And there it is," his dad said, pulling in behind a van.

They walked to a small, red-brick house. A short, blond woman came over to greet them at the door.

"So nice of you to come," she said, in a strong English accent. "I'm Fiona, Trevor's wife. I missed the game, but heard it was absolutely brilliant." She let loose with a high-pitched shriek, and then a peal of laughter. "So which one do we have here?"

"I'm Cody."

She clapped her hands to her cheeks as if shocked by the news. "I finally meet the famous striker. It is an honour."

Cody looked down at the floor.

"I'm Cheryl, and this is Sean. Thanks for doing this. It's very generous."

"Oh, please. We love it, especially after such a big win. Trevor was so nervous this morning I thought he was going to bring up his breakfast!" She let go another laugh. "Cody, your mates are downstairs destroying the basement, no doubt." She rolled her eyes and said to his mom, "I figured the best thing to do with a bunch of thirteen-year-old boys was to get them out of sight and ignore

206

them for as long as possible."

"I totally agree," his mom said. "You head on downstairs," she said to Cody. "We'll mingle up here."

He went over to the stairs. It did sound like something destructive was going on. His parents and Fiona began to talk. Fiona suddenly looked very serious, which made him feel uneasy. He took a deep breath and had barely gotten halfway down when Kenneth spotted him. He was sitting at the bottom of the stairs on the landing, with Luca and Paulo.

"Yo, Cody. What took you so long?" Paulo said.

Cody shook his head. "I went home to shower, and then we got lost . . ."

"You're the last guy here," Kenneth said. "You must be extra clean."

"*You* could've spent a bit more time in the shower," Luca joked.

Kenneth pretended to smell his armpits. He made an ugly face. "I think you're right."

Cody struggled to say something. Why couldn't he be cool like these guys?

"We were talking about the rest of the season," Kenneth said, as Cody sat on the bottom step.

"I don't think there's going to be a rest of the season," Cody said.

He must have said that too loudly because it suddenly got quiet.

"What do you mean?" Kenneth said.

"We only have eleven guys," Cody said, self-consciously. "It would be too hard without subs."

The guys began talking quietly amongst themselves. Cody leaned his elbow on his leg and rested his head in his hand. It was hard to pretend to be happy when the season was about to end before it even really started.

"Earth to Cody. Earth to Cody."

Cody looked at Kenneth. What did he want?

"So . . . how come?" Kenneth said.

"How come . . . what?"

"What I asked," Kenneth said. He sounded a little embarrassed, which was definitely strange for him.

"I might not have . . . I wasn't listening. What?. . ."

"Your hair," Paulo said. "What happened?"

Cody stuffed his hands between his knees and squeezed them tight. How could he tell them? They'd get freaked out and everything would change. He'd seen it before. As soon as he told someone he'd had cancer, they treated him like he was different.

"It's just that . . . we kinda figure . . ." Kenneth's grin was all lopsided. "We're tired of guessing. We just want to know cause you're obviously not sick."

"I wasn't so healthy about eight months ago." He tried to imitate Paulo's cockiest grin. "I had cancer treatments for a tumour in my leg. One of the side effects is you lose your hair."

It was dead quiet in the room.

"Will it grow back?" Kenneth said.

"The doctor says it will."

"And are you . . . okay now?" Luca asked.

"Of course he is; you saw him play," Kenneth said.

"They say I'll be cured if the cancer doesn't come back

for five years," Cody explained. "I guess I'll have to wait and see. The doctor thinks I should be good."

Kenneth grinned. "At least you lasted long enough for us to win the tournament," he said.

The room went quiet again.

"I say we kill Kenneth for having a big mouth," Luca said, and he grabbed a pillow from the couch and slammed Kenneth on the head.

Kenneth did a shoulder roll to get away and grabbed his own pillow. "I shall avenge myself. Attack!"

That did it. Soon all the boys were racing for pillows and cushions.

"Close the door, Trev," Cody heard Fiona say. "Let them blow off some steam."

A pillow flew by his face, missing by inches. Cody spun and picked it up just in time to ward off a wild swing from Paulo.

Paulo held his pillow over his head and said in a low voice, "Prepare to die, mortal."

Cody raised his pillow and motioned for Paulo to come closer.

★★★

A sweaty and tired crew staggered up the stairs after being summoned by Fiona. Everyone was laughing about the pillow fight and dissing one another.

"If you're so tough, why do you wear a diaper?" Luca challenged Kenneth.

"All the toughest guys wear them. I can play on the

computer all night and never have to take a bathroom break."

Luca made his fingers into guns and pointed them at Kenneth. "You might have something there, bud."

"Come into the living room, boys," Fiona called out. "We need you here to discuss something before we eat. Please. Just a minute of good behaviour."

Cody slipped in beside his parents.

"What were you doing down there?" his mom asked. "It sounded like a hurricane met up with a herd of elephants."

"Nothing much. Just fooling around."

His dad flicked his eyebrows and nudged his mom. "Now it starts. Our child doesn't tell us what he does anymore."

She squeezed Cody's arm. "That's the way it is sometimes," she said.

"While you've been having your meeting downstairs," Trevor began, and Cody laughed with his teammates, "we've been up here talking about the Lions."

"Do you mean the tournament-winning Lions?" Kenneth interrupted, and his teammates followed up with a roar.

"I don't mind being corrected about that," Trevor said. "It was a special tournament. To see you lads come together as a unit, unselfish with the ball, helping one another, all playing a role — that was as fine an example of why soccer is the beautiful game as anything I've witnessed." He held up his glass. "I had the pleasure of playing six seasons in England where I picked up a toast or two."

"Not to mention a wife," Fiona chortled.

"True enough," he said. "My favourite was taught to me

210

by an Irish lad named Danny O'Shea and it goes something like this."

All the parents in the room raised their glasses. Trevor looked around the room, his eyes seeking out each player.

May you be poor in misfortune
Rich in blessings
Slow to make enemies
Quick to make friends
But rich or poor, quick or slow
May you know nothing but happiness wherever you go.

The parents clinked their glasses, and Kenneth and Luca pretended to do the same.

"Unfortunately, as you all know, this team has a problem," Trevor said. "We only have eleven players. The period in which we can sign more players closes in a week. It would be difficult to recruit in such a short time. Without a sub we'd need every player to play every game and commit to every practice. If someone got hurt . . ." He shrugged.

Kenneth was staring straight ahead. Luca hung his head. David and Jordan, arms crossed, looked like statues.

"I know there's disappointment. I'm disappointed, too," Trevor continued.

Something welled up in Cody, too strong to stop. The idea of quitting made him sick, literally, and he'd been sick enough to last a lifetime.

"I'll play."

Cody said it just like that, quiet but firm, and all eyes turned to him.

"I appreciate the sentiment," Trevor began.

"I'll play, too," Paulo said.

Trevor sighed. "I realize . . ."

"Me, too," Kenneth said.

"And me," Luca echoed.

They wouldn't give Trevor a chance to speak. In turn, each player declared himself ready to play. Trevor rubbed his chin vigorously as he waited for the boys to finish.

"What do you think, Fi?" he said finally.

"I think the lads are trying to tell you something," Fiona said.

"What about you, Leandro? I need my manager, assistant coach, and trainer."

Leandro laughed in a clear, low tone. "I'd like to give these boys a chance to show what they can do, if they're serious."

"Are you serious?" Trevor asked aloud.

"On three, boys," Kenneth shouted. "One, two. . ."

His "three" was drowned out by a deafening roar.

Trevor held his hands out. "You've left me no choice. Practice on Tuesday, usual time. Don't be late." He paused. "And be ready to work on your fitness."

The boys all groaned, and then they began to talk at once. They were too excited to make much sense. Cody was overwhelmed. It was like getting the ten best birthday presents of his life all on the same day. Then he got an even better present. He saw his parents standing next to Fiona, and they were holding hands, his mom laughing at something his dad was saying. They looked happy.

"Who's ready for food?" Trevor asked.

"Let's do this," Kenneth said to Cody, tugging on his shirt to join the line.

"Hold on a sec. Go ahead." Cody went over to his mom and dad. "We can leave if you want. I bet Dad has some work," he said.

His dad waved him off. "Hang out as long as you want." He held up his glass. "It's all the Sprite you can drink. Why would anyone in their right mind leave?"

"Thanks," Cody said. That came out more serious than he wanted.

His mom reached out and squeezed his shoulder. There were tears in the corners of her eyes. "Don't worry about us. You go have fun with your friends," she said.

"Your mom can't leave until she's agreed to play on my women's soccer team, anyway," Fiona said. "I didn't know she was such a star — and we desperately need a striker."

"Now, stop that," his mom said.

"She's amazing," Cody said. "You gotta play, Mom."

His mom raised her eyebrows. "I just might do that," she said.

Kenneth shoved a plate into Cody's hands. "Luca would've finished all the sandwiches. I saved some just in time."

"So I'm a growing boy. Sue me," Luca said.

"We're heading downstairs," Kenneth said. "Come on."

"We'll call you when it's time to go," his mom said, and Cody followed his friends to the stairs.

MARQUIS

Québec, Canada